MW01061889

THIS BOOK BELONGS TO:

Ms. Hughes

Prairie
Winter

by Bonnie Geisert

Houghton Mifflin Books for Children
HOUGHTON MIFFLIN HARCOURT
Boston   New York   2009

Houghton Mifflin Books for Children
is an imprint of
Houghton Mifflin Harcourt Publishing Company.

www.hmhbooks.com

The text of this book is set in Garamond.
Book design by Stephanie Cooper.

Library of Congress Cataloging-in-Publication Data is on file.
ISBN 978-0-618-68588-2

Manufactured in the United States of America
MV 10 9 8 7 6 5 4 3 2 1

For Noah
and
for Gloria

Prologue

The first part of our winter, November and December of 1955, was mild in South Dakota. The temperatures were above normal, and the few snowfalls were light. But when the new year began, it became a winter that I would never forget.

Chapter 1

When the first snowfall of January came, it was sudden, heavy, and thick — giant wet flakes sauntering down, creating a curtain of white.

On the playground during noon recess we had noticed the heavy air and a dark, threatening mass of clouds to the northwest. Mrs. Kelly, our fifth- and sixth-grade teacher, was outside with us, watching the clouds. Her wrinkled brow reflected her concern.

I, too, was worried. The deepening gray in the sky signaled the possibility of a big snowstorm that would cancel school and keep me at home to work on our cattle farm.

"What's the matter, Rachel?" my friend Winnie Powers asked. "You look so disappointed."

"If this turns out to be a big storm, I'm going to be stuck at home on the farm for who knows how long. I don't like farm work in nice weather, and I *dread* it in nasty weather!" I paused for a breath. "I like school. I like being here. I like being with you and the other sixth-graders. The fifth-graders, too."

"Sorry about that," Winnie said. "If you lived in or near town, you'd love snow days. We have a lot of fun sledding, skating, and dueling it out with snowballs."

"Yeah. I can imagine the fun I'm going to miss while the wind is whipping ground corn in my face."

She tried to console me. "Well, maybe it'll be a little snowstorm."

After recess, a messenger from the school superintendent's office knocked on the classroom door. I held my breath when Mrs. Kelly went to open it. Twenty-three fifth- and sixth-grade pairs of ears tuned in to the voice outside the door. It said what I feared. "We're going to dismiss . . ."

At those words, many in the room clapped their hands — softly. Mrs. Kelly would not tolerate rowdiness. Winnie stood and motioned for silence in order to hear the rest of the message. ". . . phone call from the sheriff's office in Faulkton, warning of heavy snow approaching north-central South Dakota." We leaned forward in our seats toward the voice. "Several inches are already on the ground in Bowdle . . ."

Bowdle is only about fifty miles from Cresbard! I thought.

". . . and traffic is not advised. As soon as all the bus drivers are in, we'll ring the dismissal bell and the kids should go immediately to their buses or home."

"This doesn't surprise me," Mrs. Kelly replied to the unseen messenger outside the door. "The weather forecast didn't sound good on the radio this morning." When she closed the door, we sat back in our seats, waiting for her announcement.

"We will be dismissing early," she said. Her voice, usually calm, sounded urgent. "There's some heavy snow expected, and we want to get you home before it starts, so clear your desks and be ready when the bell rings. As soon as the buses are lined up, we'll dismiss."

I raised my hand. After Mrs. Kelly nodded to me, I asked, "Do you think we'll have school tomorrow?"

"That depends on how much snow we get, Rachel."

"I hope not very much," I replied softly.

She smiled. She knew how much I loved school and everything about it.

"Look! It's starting!" Lance Cooper exclaimed. All heads turned toward the wall of windows.

"Look at those big snowflakes!" Melissa Powers, Winnie's cousin, said.

We all started toward the windows for a closer look.

"Remain in your seats, boys and girls!" reminded Mrs. Kelly. Everyone sat down except Lance, who often tried to get away with stuff. He stayed by his seat near the window but continued to stand, looking out, then sitting down just as Mrs. Kelly started to reprimand him. "Lance . . ."

A minute of quiet waiting followed. The ticking of the clock was the loudest sound in the room.

Claaaang!

The sound of the bell hammer hitting against its metal casing in the hall startled us.

Mrs. Kelly took a final survey of her students to make sure we all were ready for dismissal. "Row one, you may go," she said.

"Row two." All the fifth-graders rose and walked out.

"Row three." My row got up. "And row four."

We hurried down to the stairway landing, where our coats hung on metal hooks above our boots. It was hard to keep our excited, anxious voices down as we put on coats, caps, scarves, and overshoes.

I zipped up my gray wool jacket with its fur collar and embroidered front edges — a hand-me-down from older sisters — Carol, fifteen, and Kim, thirteen. I tied my plaid wool scarf under my chin, pulled on my overshoes, and zipped them to the top of the fur trim a few inches above my ankles.

Those of us who were band members grabbed our instrument cases. We were supposed to practice every night for a big concert coming up in Chicago next year. I grasped the handle of my coronet case so it wouldn't slip from my hands when I ran to the bus.

Mrs. Kelly stood at the top of the stairway by the classroom door, making sure we got off okay. "Goodbye, Mrs. Kelly," we all called up to her.

"Hope to see you tomorrow," I added.

"I hope so, too." She smiled briefly, and then the worried look returned to her face.

We didn't *run* down the stairs to the first floor, but we weren't exactly walking, either. We passed third- and fourth-graders on their way to the door. Outside, we saw the five buses, with their motors running, lined up on the west side of the schoolyard.

Everyone took off, running toward the buses. Some of the older kids leaped over the board fence, and some of the younger ones took a shortcut under it, disregarding the safety rule of going only through the walkway opening.

The snow was already more than an inch deep, and footprint pressed upon footprint created a path of packed, slippery snow that narrowed at the gate.

I was almost to that point when a powerful *whomp* hit me on the back. Wet snow splattered over my shoulders and melted around my neck.

"Wha . . ." Stunned, I turned around and ducked just in time to avoid the next snowball hurling toward my head. In the heavy falling snow I could barely see the culprit. *I should have known!* "Just you wait, Lance Cooper!" I yelled to him as he left the schoolyard with the town kids who walked home.

He laughed, not intimidated at all. "Wait for what, Rachel Johnson?" He tossed another snowball that fell short. Then he turned and strolled down the street toward his house.

I would have to wait to seek my revenge another time.

For now, I was concerned about how long it would take to get home. The houses near the school had faded into faint rectangular forms, almost invisible through the white world of falling snow.

Chapter 2

"You boys are going to wish you had galoshes on!" Les, our bus driver, said when a couple of the high-schoolers, wearing wet loafers, boarded.

"Galoshes are so uncool, Les," one answered. "Besides, we didn't know it was going to snow today."

"It's winter." Les smiled. "It snows in winter — and this is going to be a big snow, they say. Can hardly see the houses over there." He pointed toward the houses half a block away.

When it looked like all the kids were boarded on the buses, Les swung the handle that closed the door halves together. "Everyone seated!" he commanded, and he checked in his rearview mirror to make sure before he disengaged the clutch and rolled out behind the other buses.

I waved when I saw Winnie and Melissa's bus turn left. Winnie lived only a half mile east of town, and Melissa lived half a mile north of Winnie. I couldn't see if they waved back — the space between the buses was too white.

They *will be home soon. But not me,* I thought. I was envious that they would be able to get together and have fun if there were no school tomorrow. Susie, my little seven-year-old sister, who was in second-grade and huddled next to me, wouldn't be nearly as much fun as Winnie and Melissa. *Winnie and Melissa will probably get to go tobogganing with Lance and Darren like they did last weekend.* Lance was a pill, but Darren Baxter was one cool guy.

I looked out the window over Susie's head. Our bus traveled south down Main Street. Only a few cars were in town, and most of those were parked in front of the mercantile store, the grocery store, and the gas station. We drove beneath the Christmas lights that crossed the main intersection downtown — still up, though Christmas was more than a week ago. We left Main Street, the grain elevators, and the livestock sale barn at the edge of town and traveled the mile to Highway 20, the east–west main gravel road.

The snow was so thick in the air that I couldn't see Herbie Conlon's hangar and landing strip, though they were only about a hundred feet from the road, in the alfalfa field paralleling it.

When Les turned the bus onto Highway 20, the tracks left behind on the road were firmly pressed into deepening snow. Distinct patterns from the tire chains left large chain-link depressions in the center of the tire tracks. The power-line poles along the road were packed with snow on the north sides. Everything was white, and it was hard to see the road between the ditches that ran alongside it.

At the pace we were going, it would take a long time to get home. Our farm was only eight miles from town, but the bus route would cover twenty miles and six stops before Carol, Kim, Susie, and I were dropped off. We had gone only one mile so far.

After each stop, the footprints left by the kids getting off were deeper than the stop before. If the farm was down a lane, the house might not be in sight.

At the Kahn farm, where one very small boy and girl lived, Les opened the door and peered out. He hesitated, as though he didn't want them to get off. I looked out the window and saw nothing but swirling snow. *How will they find their house?*

"Dick! Devon!" Les beckoned to Dick Mackey and Devon Hart. The two oldest boys on the bus hurried to the front.

What does he want them for? I wondered.

In the whiteness, something appeared to move toward the bus. The something turned gray and started to resemble a person. Then the solid form of a heavily clad figure emerged.

"Les!" a voice called. Les opened the door.

"Karl! Boy am I glad to see you!" Les exclaimed when Mr. Kahn stepped inside the bus. "I didn't feel right about letting your two little ones out in this snow without your house in sight. I was thinking of sending Dick and Devon to make sure they got to the door, but then I'd have to worry about them, too."

"We heard the radio announcement about school letting out early," Mr. Kahn said. "I was waiting earlier, but when you didn't come, I went back to the house to see if the radio had further news."

"It's been slow going," Les said. "The snow is getting deep. Okay, Chip and Megan, you can get off now."

"Good luck to you, Les!" Mr. Kahn said, and he stepped

down from the bus with Chip and Megan. Holding each child by the hand, he headed back toward his house. The bus pulled away slowly, and Mr. Kahn, Chip, and Megan disappeared into the whiteness.

Now there were three more stops and eleven more miles to our farm. At the next stop, to my surprise, the snow was lighter. I could see that house even though it was a distance from the road.

My ears perked up when I heard Carol, who was sitting with Maureen Mackey behind Susie and me, say, "This storm reminds me of the end of *Giants in the Earth*."

"You're reading that now in English class, huh?" Maureen answered. "We read it last year, too."

"Would you have gone out in that storm, like Per Hansa did, if you thought you couldn't survive it?" Carol asked.

"I don't know. If he hadn't gone, can you imagine how his wife, Beret, would have felt about him if their friend Hans Olsa had died without a minister? She was so sure that he would die in sin and go to hell."

"It was *evident* that Hans Olsa was going to die, but only *possible* that Per Hansa would," said Carol. "Beret might never have forgiven him."

"How sad the ending was," Maureen said. "I almost

cried when I read that they found Per Hansa in the spring, sitting with his back against an old haystack. Dead. His skis still on."

"I would have preferred a different ending . . ." Carol shook her head.

I would, too! I thought, not waiting for her to finish.

". . . but things were tough for the Norwegian immigrants in the late eighteen hundreds."

"To think that *Giants in the Earth* was set right *here* in South Dakota," added Maureen.

Carol nodded. "The author was Norwegian, and he visited his uncle in South Dakota. We still have a lot of Norwegian descendants today, especially in the southeastern part of the state."

That explains those funny names, I thought. *Per Hansa. Hans Olsa. They're Norwegian names!*

What relief I felt when I next looked out the window. The snow had stopped — almost as suddenly as it had started. Travel was still slow, but we could see the road, and that helped our speed.

I began to relax. Susie, too, for she no longer pressed against me in the seat. There was even a little space between us.

The Mackeys were the last ones off before us.

"Okay, girls," Les said, looking in his rearview mirror at us as he left the Mackey farm. "I should have no problem getting you home."

"Good!" Susie said.

Relieved, I smiled at his reflection. Carol and Kim sat back in their seats.

"I wonder if Mom got home," I said. Fifteen-month-old Matthew had been crying and pulling at his ear in the morning, so Mom was taking him to the doctor in Faulkton.

"I hope Dad got home from the livestock sale," Carol said. "The road won't be cleared in time to take the car, so I'll need him to take me to town in the truck. I *promised* Gretchen that I would be there tonight for cheerleading, and the basketball bus leaves at five-thirty."

"That seems like a silly promise in weather like this," I said. "Promises are sacred. They are supposed to be saved for important things."

"Well, who are you? Little Miss Know It All?" Kim mocked.

"Just putting in my two cents."

"It's more like one cent."

"Stop putting me down, Kim —"

"It *was* a silly promise," Carol interrupted. "But Gretchen is my best friend, and the other two cheerleaders weren't sure they could make it in."

"Gretchen lives in town, so it's easier for her to get to the bus," I pointed out.

"Yeah, like that isn't obvious?" Kim snickered.

"Hey, leave me alone!"

"*I* wouldn't want to cheerlead by myself," Carol said, "so just in case no one else shows, I will."

Carol was such a loyal friend to Gretchen. I wondered if Gretchen would have been that loyal to her. And Carol had character. If she made a promise, she kept it. That was one of the qualities — along with her nice personality and her athletic ability — that got her elected to the cheerleading squad. Kim, too, as a junior high cheerleader. Making the squad next year, when I would be in junior high, was one of my dreams.

At our mile turnoff, I noticed car tracks in the snow that had turned in from the road to Faulkton. I didn't see any truck tracks from the other direction.

Most likely, Dad had not made it home.

Chapter 3

When Les turned into our lane, there was, again, only one set of tracks. He drove up on the cement drive to the garage, just as the car tracks had, but the tracks disappeared under the garage door.

When the bus stopped, Susie was first to the door. "It's cold!" she said.

"The temperature has definitely fallen," Les said.

I felt it, too. I checked the thermometer near the house door. "Fifteen degrees!" I called to Les.

"That's thirteen degrees colder than when we left school. That's quite a drop," he said. "Good night, girls!" he called before he closed the door and backed away.

The bus had no more riders, so Les could return directly to school on the county road.

Blackie came bounding out of the chicken coop when he heard our voices.

"Sorry, Blackie! No time for petting today," I apologized. I wanted to see how Mom and Matthew were.

"Hi, Mom! How's Matthew?" I asked when we walked into the kitchen.

"He's sleeping," she said in a low voice. "Don't wake him, Susie," she warned when Susie headed for the bedroom where his crib was. "He's been fussy, but the doctor prescribed some medicine for an ear infection that also makes him sleepy, and the sleep's good for him."

"Did you have to drive in the storm, Mom?" I asked. "We could hardly see out the bus for the first few miles."

"I heard on the radio that school was getting out early. The snow was heavy in Faulkton but must not have been as heavy as you had. I'm glad we have the Oldsmobile. It's a big car and hugs the road well, but I had to go slow. There were times when I thought it would get stuck on me."

"I hope Dad gets home soon," Carol said. "I promised Gretchen I'd make it tonight for cheerleading."

"Silly promise," I said.

Carol ignored me, but Kim didn't. "You already said that, Rachel!"

"Girls!" Mom scolded. "Carol, if there was snow toward Aberdeen, like there was in Cresbard, Dad could be late," Mom pointed out.

"The bus leaves at five-thirty!" Carol insisted. "If Dad's not here at four-thirty, I'm taking the car."

I looked at the clock above the window. So did Mom. The hands pointed to 3:45. Daylight was beginning to fade.

Mom was upset by Carol's determination, and I wondered what she would do.

In the silence of that moment, waiting for Mom's ultimatum, we heard a dreaded winter sound.

"The wind!" Mom gasped.

Looking out, we saw thick white wisps. The wind was sweeping the snow across the fields. If that kept up, drifts would form across the road and block it. Dad would have to drive slowly. If there were whiteouts, he'd have to stop until he could see out the windshield again.

"Even if Dad makes it by four-thirty, I don't think he's going to take you back to town in this weather, Carol," Mom said. She moved to the window to check the temperature on the thermometer near the door. "Twelve degrees!" she exclaimed. "It's going to get much colder by nightfall."

Then, without explanation, she opened the kitchen door and walked down the three steps and out into the breezeway. We heard the garage door open and looked at each other with questioning eyes. Then we heard the car door.

"She's taking the keys out of the car!" Carol exclaimed.

"That won't stop me, Mom!" Carol declared when Mom returned. "I promised. Gretchen *made* me promise. You have to *keep* a promise."

"Gretchen has no idea what you have promised. She doesn't realize the danger. She lives in town. They may well decide to cancel the ball game in weather like this," Mom said.

This is when a phone would come in handy, I thought. But when any of us brought it up, Mom would say, "Don't start!" There was no changing Dad's mind. He was as obstinate about not having a phone as Carol was about keeping her promise. Dad assumed that we girls would be on the phone all the time if we had one. He was right in my case. It would be my connection to the kids in town. And Dad always claimed that phones never worked in an emergency. Why he said that, I don't know. There were two miles of line, also, to our nearest neighbor with a phone that he'd have to pay for if we did decide to get a telephone.

"A promise is a promise! People don't trust someone who breaks a promise. We learned that in confirmation class at church," Carol announced. "I'll *walk* to town!"

"Eight miles?" Kim asked. "You won't make it in an hour."

"Somebody will come along and give me a ride."

"In *this* weather?" Mom asked, stretching her height to match her oldest daughter's. "Carol, for heaven's sake, I have a sick baby in the other room. Look at the blowing snow! You know how dangerous the wind is in frigid weather like this."

Carol turned away. "I have to go!"

"I'm your mother! You are supposed to obey me. You learned *that* when you learned the Ten Commandments! That's more important than a promise."

Carol hesitated. "No it isn't!" she said, and then left for her room.

With shoulders slumped, Mom rested her frame on the kitchen stool.

I went to Carol's room. "Carol, how can you go out in weather like this? I heard you and Maureen talking about *Giants in the Earth* on the bus. Don't you remember what happened to Per Hansa?"

"That's fiction, Rachel," she replied. She pulled on a pair of slacks under her skirt.

"It seemed so real, Carol. I don't want *you* to get lost and freeze to death like he did."

"Fiction!" She pulled a pair of socks over the anklets she was wearing and buttoned a cardigan over her sweater. "Per Hansa had twenty inches of snow to deal with. Do you see twenty inches of snow out there?" When she finished bundling up, she had a wool scarf and a pair of gloves over mittens, and her clothes were securely buttoned into her new winter coat — a style they called storm coat.

"Carol, please. I beg you!" Mom tried one last time before Carol reached the kitchen door. "If you go . . ."

Carol looked at her, waiting for Mom to finish her sentence. When she didn't, she left the kitchen and stepped down into the breezeway.

I ran after her. "Carol, please!"

She zipped up her overshoes and walked out the door.

From the big living room window, Susie and I watched Carol walking down the road. We saw her bundled gray form, swirled by white, follow the bend in the road. Kim and Mom stood behind us. The wind raged and blew snow against and around solid objects. We watched, silent, until Carol disappeared into the wall of white.

Mom collapsed in Dad's recliner. I'd never seen her eyes look so sad.

I was afraid we would never see Carol again.

We took turns at vigil, even after dark. No sign of Dad or Carol. I couldn't get the picture of Per Hansa out of my mind. His form turned into Carol's. *She* was sitting with *her* back against a haystack. There were haystacks, like there were in *Giants in the Earth,* in our field next to the county road, too. *Carol* was frozen and covered with snow, not to be found until spring, still bundled in her new storm coat.

The night dragged on. For hours we looked out the window for a sign of lights appearing in the night. Then, just before midnight, we saw light beams on the road.

"That has to be your dad!" Mom declared. "Who else would be on this road at this time of night? Unless . . ."

"Unless *what?*" I asked.

"Nothing," she said.

But I was sure that I knew what she was thinking.

Our eyes followed the slow-moving lights and watched them turn into our lane.

"Please let that be Tony," Mom said. "Oh, please let Carol be with him!"

"It's the pickup, Mom!" Kim exclaimed as it passed the window.

"It's Dad!" I cried out. "I think Carol's with him, too!"

She didn't freeze to death!

Mom went out to the garage to open the door for the pickup. Kim, Susie, and I followed. Relief flooded through us when the garage lights revealed both Dad and Carol in the pickup cab.

"You, young lady, have put me through one of the worst nights of my life!" Mom scolded Carol when she got out of the pickup. "But I don't think I've ever been so relieved to see you.

"And you!" she said to Dad. "Did she tell you what she did?" Mom asked him. "That she walked away from here in the storm, against my wishes?"

"She didn't give me all the details, but I wondered," he said. "When I stopped in town to see if the ball game had been canceled, Will Hall was there and told me that she had knocked on his door, half frozen."

She only made it two miles! I thought.

Mom took Dad's big parka and hung it on the nail in

the garage for him while he pulled off his boots in the breezeway. She closed the garage door and kept shaking her head.

Carol walked past Mom into the house. Her head was down, and she didn't look at any of us.

"Why didn't Will bring her home?" Mom asked.

"He wanted to, but Carol only wanted to warm up before she went on," Dad continued. "She was determined to walk to town, so he put some hay bales in his pickup for traction and he took her to meet the bus."

She would not have survived the eight miles. There were no more houses along the road that led to town to stop and warm up in!

"Will decided to stay in case she needed a ride home," Dad went on. "I thanked him, apologized for my stubborn daughter, who I said takes after me, and said I would wait for her."

"Aren't you mad at her?" Kim demanded. "You sure would be if it was me!"

"Or me!" I added.

"We'll deal with Carol," Dad said. "She knows she put herself in unnecessary danger."

"And me through *un*necessary worry," Mom said.

"Me, too. I thought she was going to freeze to death," I said.

"You did not!" Kim accused.

"I did so, Kim!"

"Girrrls!" Mom snapped.

"I scolded her on the way home between snowdrifts," Dad said. "She won't do that again."

"There's still the matter of disobeying her mother!" Mom said.

"Yes, that will be addressed," Dad agreed. "For now, let's get to bed and get some sleep. There will be a lot of snow to shovel tomorrow."

Oh, please let there be school tomorrow! I prayed.

Chapter 4

"There will be no school in Cresbard today."

"Oh no!" I groaned softly when the radio announcement floated into the bedroom. That meant work — hard work. We'd have to shovel snow, feed cattle, and anything else that Dad *thought* was necessary.

I rolled on my side, facing Susie — still sound asleep — and pulled the covers over my head. *I'm not getting up until they make me.*

The early morning light passing through the east window told me that it was about seven-thirty. I knew I would not be lying in bed much longer.

The radio news continued for a few minutes, followed by a repeat of school closings. All schools in Faulk County were closed. When the country music came on, the volume was turned down and I heard Dad ask Mom, "Are any of the girls up, Kid?"

"I don't hear anyone stirring," she replied. Mom was rattling pots and pans and dishes in the kitchen, getting breakfast ready. Dad was probably sitting at the table with a cup of coffee, listening to the news and planning the work for the day.

"We have lots of snow to shovel today and the cattle to feed," Dad said.

"I imagine Carol is pretty tired after walking in that blowing snow last night — and the rest of us didn't get any sleep until you made it home," Mom said.

"I guess we can let them sleep a few more minutes." Coming from Dad, that was a surprise.

"Carol had better not pull that again!" Mom said. "There was no stopping her. She had that promise to keep, no matter what. Remember those children in North Dakota a few years ago?" she continued. "I kept thinking about them last night. They never did make it home from school in that blizzard."

"Carol said that she'll be careful about the promises she makes in the future," Dad said. "Last night was a tough way to learn that lesson. Thank God it had a safe ending."

"Amen to that!" Mom said. "I think grounding her from the next four ball games is fair. What do you think?" Mom asked.

Carol loves cheerleading! I was sort of sorry to hear that, but she deserved it.

"Just four?" Dad said. "Don't you think you're being a little easy on her?"

"Just four. *And* an apology. How's that?" Mom said.

"Sounds very fair to me."

Apologizing and admitting you were wrong is hard. I hope I'm around when she does it. Still, she's getting off easy.

Their talking stopped. Only the radio music and kitchen sounds were heard in my room.

Then I heard Dad planning. "The feed for the fat cattle is getting a little low, come to think of it. We should probably grind some corn today."

Oh no, not grinding corn. I hope that's not one of my jobs!

I listened for the wind. All the chores would be complicated by the wind, especially grinding corn. It must not have been blowing hard, because I couldn't hear it. I hoped that wouldn't change.

I heard Dad's chair scrape the floor when he pushed it back. I knew that probably meant he was going to get us out of bed. "Breakfast about ready, Kid?" he asked Mom.

"In just a few minutes," she replied.

He went first to Carol and Kim's room. "Up and at 'em!" he called, knocking on their closed door. "We have work to do! There's no school today, and"— groans came from their bedroom —"breakfast is almost ready! By the way, Carol, for disobeying your mother, you will miss the next four ball games, and you must apologize to her for your disregard of her authority."

No reply was heard from Carol.

"If you can't do that, then you will miss the next eight ball games," Dad threatened.

"Okay," she growled.

"And your apology will not have attitude!"

His footsteps came down the hall toward our room. I closed my eyes, pretending to be asleep.

"Up and at 'em!" he called again, standing outside our open door. "Mom has breakfast almost ready."

I opened my eyes. Susie stirred beneath the covers.

"No school today," he announced, "but there's plenty to do here." He smiled directly at me. He knew that I was not a farmer at heart. "Lots of snow to shovel! Gotta hay the cattle in the yards and in the pasture. Grind some corn. We're gonna have so much fun today that you'll wish you'd never have to go back to school again!" he said, laughing.

That will be when hell freezes over. I didn't dare say that out loud, because Dad would consider that swearing and sass. I simply rolled my eyes at him.

"Hey, Susie! Wake up!" He came to the bed and gently shook the pillow under her head.

"Don't!" Susie said. Sometimes she was cranky when she first woke up.

"Five minutes!" Mom called from the kitchen.

"Everyone up. Meet you at the table!" Dad said.

My first assignment, and Kim's, was to pitch hay for the cattle in the pasture across the creek from the farmyard. Kim and I bundled up from head to toe, for the temperature was a frigid minus five degrees. We walked through snow ten inches deep, our pitchforks in hand.

We crossed the frozen creek to get to the barn-size haystack in the pasture. I noticed large areas on the creek that had been swept clear of snow by the wind. *Great for skating. I hope we get our chores done, so I have some time to skate.* That was a good reason for me to pitch the hay faster than

I normally would. That, and the cold, would encourage me to move.

When we neared the stack, the cattle scattered from their huddle. They had eaten holes so deep into the stack that even with their long necks, they couldn't reach the hay inside the stack corral. Kim and I pitched hay from the top so it filled the gaping holes. The cattle quickly moved in and started eating.

When the holes were full, we retraced our steps and did the same at the other haystacks in the two separate barnyards.

I was tired. My face was numb, and I couldn't feel it when I wrinkled my nose or tried to smile.

"Come on up to the house!" Dad hollered from the high point in the center of the farmyard, where he and Carol were standing. They had been shoveling snow from garage doors, barn doors, and corncrib doors, and clearing the drive and lane with the hydraulic scoop — we called it a farmhand — attached to the tractor.

Dad repeated the call with a beckoning wave.

"We're coming!" Kim yelled back.

"A break at last," I said to Kim as we climbed down the haystack.

"You don't really need one. You didn't do much."

"I did, too!"

"Not really."

"Well, if I didn't, it's because I'm not as big as you are!"

Kim didn't say anything else on the way to the house.

The bologna on buttered bread, peanut butter cookies, and hot cocoa that Mom had waiting for us was appreciated all the way from my nose and tongue to my stomach. The warmth of the kitchen brought tingling to my face and painful stings to my fingers and toes. Too soon it was time to go back outside.

To clear the yard and lane, Dad continued scraping piles of snow into the hydraulic scoop, then pushing, lifting, and dumping snow into mounds in out-of-the-way places while Kim, Carol, and I finished pitching hay.

Grinding the corn followed. The wind was blowing — not howling, but blowing enough to swirl the fine kernel and cob particles as they shot from the grinder into the feed wagon. Carol was the unlucky sister who had to protect her eyes from the invading kernel and cob specks.

My job, and Kim's, was kicking the ears of corn from their bed in the crib to the opening in the slats, where Dad collected them into his grain scoop and tossed them into the grinder, which pulverized the ears into golden yellow powdery feed. The ears did not slide easily over one another, nor did they willingly obey a grain shovel, but the heels and toes of my cowboy boots digging and kicking at them got the ears to the opening, where Dad could reach them.

It seemed that the feed wagon was taking forever to fill today, and I was eager to go ice-skating. But finally the wagon was full and the chores were declared done.

I carried my polished white ice skates to a special section of the creek. Blackie ran along beside me with his usual enthusiasm. He would chase off after something in the snow once I started skating. The light was fading in the late afternoon, so I quickly laced the strings up the notches. I was the only one in the family who skated. Carol and Kim weren't interested, Susie not much, either, so I did it alone. There was something about the grace and fluid motion of gliding, first on one foot and then the other, that made me feel so good, so carefree, as if I were dancing. I dreamed of being a ballerina when I grew up, and in my mind, I was a ballerina while skating.

My ice-skating rink — my stage — was a long, wide section of the creek with high bluffs on both sides. Sometimes I had an audience — a group of cattle that gathered at the top of the bluffs. They usually did not wander down when I was there. I didn't feel as intimidated by them as I did when I was younger. Still, I knew firsthand their unpredictable behavior, especially if they were new cattle from the wide-open ranges of western South Dakota and North Dakota, Montana, and Wyoming — places where Dad had a tendency to buy our stock.

I skated until the light faded — until I heard Mom call, "Rachel! Suppertime!" Her voice sang through the cold, dense air.

"Okay!" I yelled back, assuming she would hear me, too, across the three hundred yards up and over the hill. I couldn't resist a couple more glides and turns around my arena. I did not want to stop and end this wonderful feeling. I was tempted to try a jump, but I wasn't brave enough. With my luck, I would probably fall and hurt myself.

I unlaced my skates, slipped into my cold shoes that still sat in my overshoes, slung the skates over my shoulder, and trudged through the snow to the house.

Dusk had given way to evening darkness, and the light from the kitchen window cast a warm glow on the ground. I hurried when I saw my family sitting around the table.

Chapter 5

The next morning, to my joy, school was open again. The town kids, including Winnie, Melissa, and Lance, talked about all the fun they'd had the day before, tobogganing on the slopes of Cresbard Lake and snowball fighting. They had built sturdy snow forts on the school ground as retreats for when the snowballs were flying fast and furious.

Hearing about it made me realize the good time I had missed. How I wished that I lived in town and could join the excitement! We lived so far out that if it weren't for school, Saturday nights, and Sunday mornings, my life would be a total bore.

The temperature had warmed up by noon recess, making the snow perfect for snowballs. Several of us chased away the third- and fourth-graders from the forts, reclaiming them for the fifth- and sixth-graders who were game for a snowball fight.

"Boys against the girls!" Lance called, packing snow in his gloved hands.

"You're on!" Winnie said.

"Yeah! You boys better run for cover behind the fort!" I sneered. We were all packing loose snowballs and aiming them at shoulders, backs — generally below the head.

"You girls don't stand a chance!" David boasted. "You throw like girls!" Then he threw a slow, sloppy one that broke up on the ground in front of us in mockery.

Splat! A fast one caught Winnie off-guard right on the side of her head.

"Ouch!" she cried, feeling the spot where the snow left its mark on her head scarf.

"Lance! You jerk!" I yelled. "Below the head! That's the rule!"

"War!" he yelled back. "We just declared war, and all's fair in love and war!" He fired a fast one before I could duck, and it hit me in the neck.

"Ouch! Time out!" I yelled.

"No time-outs! War!" Lance whooped.

When we girls realized that the boys were going to fight dirty, we retreated behind our fort.

"Make lots of snowballs, and don't throw them until they attack us over here. Then we'll bombard them with a volley of snowballs!" I said.

There were five of us forming snowballs as fast as we could. By the time the boys approached in a supposed sneak attack, each of us had a pile beside us, ready to throw.

We laughed as they ran for cover behind their fort wall, bombarded by snowballs all the way. "Take that! And that!" we yelled, chasing after them.

"And that!" Winnie said, hitting Lance in the back of the head before he ducked behind the wall.

"Attagirl, Winnie!" I congratulated her.

"Bull's-eye!" Melissa shouted.

We were so pleased with Winnie's shot that we didn't see Lance rise above his wall and return a snowball to Winnie. It smacked her right in the eye.

"Ow!" She winced, covering her eye with her hand.

"Lance! You creep!" I yelled. "Let me see, Winnie!"

Her eye was red, and swelling started to form, so that she could hardly open it.

"Ewww," she groaned.

"Oh, my, Winnie!" Melissa said. "Wait until Mrs. Kelly sees this!" she warned Lance.

"Tattletales!" he yelled.

"I don't know, Lance. Look at her eye," David said. He had walked near to see for himself. He was a little sweet on Winnie and seemed sincerely concerned.

"Winnie, let's go in and have Mrs. Kelly take a look. It's really swelling up," I said, guiding her by her elbow toward the door. Her eyelid was now swollen over half of her right eye.

"Does it hurt?" David asked.

"It stings," she admitted.

"Uh-oh!" Lance said regretfully.

"Yeah! You'll get yours!" I replied.

Melissa and I accompanied Winnie to our room, where we found Mrs. Kelly correcting papers at her desk.

"Mrs. Kelly, look at Winnie's eye! It got hit by a snowball and it's swelling," I said. I was sure she would ask who threw it, so I didn't tattle.

"Oh, my, it sure is!" she said. "One of you girls get a damp, cold paper towel from the restroom, and that should help a little with the swelling."

Melissa ran after it.

"Who threw the snowball?" Mrs. Kelly asked.

"Lance did!" I said, pleased at the opportunity to tell on him. Not only was he a pill, but I think I had it in for him. At the beginning of the school year, he had announced that he liked Melissa instead of me.

Melissa returned with the cold paper towel, and Winnie held it over her eye.

"Recess is almost over, girls. You might as well take off your coats and stay in the room," Mrs. Kelly suggested.

The bell rang shortly after that, and soon everyone was seated and ready to start afternoon classes.

Before the lessons began, Mrs. Kelly stood in front of the room and looked directly at Lance Cooper as she said, "It appears that some of you are going to have to practice your aim if you don't want snowball fights to be outlawed on school grounds."

"She hit me in the head first!" a guilty Lance protested.

Mrs. Kelly suddenly grew six inches taller. "Any more outbursts like that and snowballs will be outlawed for this class immediately!" she declared. She paused, poised at her don't-argue-with-me height. I was certain there would be no other outbursts. I loved Mrs. Kelly because she was a good teacher, and she was fair and had a sense of humor. She was also strict and didn't put up with any nonsense.

Winnie's swollen eye and Mrs. Kelly's reaction cooled our snowball fights for the next few days. Instead, we played fox-and-goose tag. It wasn't quite as exciting, but it had its moments. And there was plenty of snow for it.

Whoever suggested the game led the rest of us in trampling a large circle in the snow. Then we made three diagonal paths across the circle, making it look like a huge wheel with six spokes. In the center we trampled a small, solid circle as the safe base. All the "geese" would stand there while the "fox" waited for his opportunity to catch a goose or two or three that might dare to run down one of the paths. A tagged goose became a fox and helped catch other geese.

Whenever Lance was the fox, I could count on him to give me a hard time and call foul play whenever I escaped his attempts.

"You went off the path, Johnson!" Lance called me by my last name when he was irked at me, and staying on the paths at all times was a major rule.

"I *did* not!" I had just outrun him around the perimeter and dashed into base. "You are such a spoilsport!"

"You did, too!"

"Where's my footprint?" I demanded.

"Yeah! Where's her footprint?" Winnie yelled beside me. Then she took off, daring him to chase her down a path.

Melissa, David, and a few others were baiting Lance from various points around the perimeter.

"See? Right here is your footprint!" Lance pointed to a heel mark near the edge of a path.

"Let it go, Lance!" Darren Baxter said.

Darren, who seemed to like me, had started hanging around with Lance and David. I thought he was cute. And he was smart. Lance had tagged him earlier, so he had become another fox and now helped catch the geese.

"Catch me if you can," Melissa sang out.

Lance turned and started slowly edging himself down a path toward her. She moved away from him around the perimeter. He took a sudden sprint, and when she ran, she bumped into a slower girl in front of her who blocked her getaway.

"Gotcha!" Lance cried when he tagged her.

Melissa laughed. She didn't seem to care. Lance had not slammed her hard on her back as he would have if he had caught me.

"Okay, foxy Lancy, catch *me* if you can!" I taunted. I had moved from the center down one of the paths to the opposite side of the perimeter.

Three foxes were now chasing, and the game heated up. Melissa and Darren went after David and trapped him. Those three teamed up and caught three more. Winnie and I were the only ones left. We'd stay free geese as long as we could or until the bell rang.

There was no way, I decided, that I would allow Lance to tag me. I could see that he was planning a strategy. I had a strategy of my own, and that was to let Darren catch me so Lance couldn't. I ran away from Lance in Darren's direction. Lance darted toward me, shoving one of the girls off the path so he wouldn't step off. I was about halfway between Lance and Darren. I hesitated, thought better of just giving up and letting Darren tag me, and I turned into a path free of foxes and made it to base.

"Are you going to stay there till the bell rings, Johnson?" Lance jeered.

"We got Winnie!" David boasted.

"She probably let you catch her." Lance smirked.

"No I didn't!" Winnie declared.

Winnie went to Melissa and whispered something in her ear. Melissa whispered it to the girl beside her and then whispered it to a fourth girl in the pie. Each girl moved to a location that hemmed Lance in.

Yeah! I thought. *Winnie is so clever! Lance wouldn't dare knock one of the girls off a path with everyone watching.* I gave the girls a beaming smile of appreciation.

"Rachel! Rachel!" the girls began chanting.

"You can't do this!" Lance protested.

"Show us the rule book, buster!" Winnie demanded.

With Lance blocked, I now had to evade Darren *and* David. They had closed in near the base on two of the spokes. They realized this goose wouldn't leave her henhouse with foxes that close, so they moved out closer to the perimeter, hoping to bait me.

Hmm! I have few options. The option of staying here and waiting for the bell is unsporting. No honor in that!

"You're chicken, Johnson!" Lance yelled.

I ignored his taunt. I needed to concentrate on a strategy. There wasn't much time left, and I didn't want it to look like I was stalling. There were two free spokes to one side of the ones occupied by the two boys. I saw a way to evade them. I ran out in the path farthest from them, knowing they would both dash after me. I was sure I could outrace them around the perimeter and back to the first free spoke, and end up safe at base.

"Go, Rachel, go!" the girls cheered from their spokes.

I took small, swift steps to avoid missing the curved path. David was closing in behind me. I couldn't run into the first two spokes, because they were blocked with girls blocking Lance.

Oh, jeepers! Darren was racing around the perimeter in the opposite direction, speeding toward me.

I heard David grunt behind me.

"Turn around, Rachel!" the girls yelled. "David ran off the path!"

My short steps served me well. It was easier to reverse my direction without losing precious time. But Darren was just feet away and had the edge of full speed ahead, when, unfortunately, I had to slow down to turn around.

I knew he was getting close when the girls hollered, "Run, Rachel, run!"

I did. With all my might! The bell rang, but I kept on running. I was determined to reach base. When I did, I looked back for Darren and saw him laughing in the perimeter.

"Hey, the bell rang!" he said. "Game's over!"

"Good! I'm out of breath!" Leaning with my hands on my knees, I waited until my breathing slowed.

With excited voices we replayed the game all the way to the school door.

Chapter 6

When the January thaw came in the middle of the month, it melted the snow, crumpled the snow forts, shortened the snowmen into sagging forms, and erased the fox-and-goose pie. The playground became wet and soggy.

At home, our barnyards were a mushy brown and cattle walked ankle-deep in muck.

One morning when the temperature was especially warm, Carol, Kim, and I were about to walk out the door to the bus without our heavy coats and overshoes, when Mom stopped us.

"Take your winter coats and overshoes with you," she said.

"But it's so warm," Kim complained.

"Yeah," I agreed.

"You should remember how quickly that storm came up earlier this month," Mom reminded us. "The radio hinted of another possible storm brewing."

"Ra — chel," Susie called weakly from our bedroom. She had been complaining about stomachaches for the past few days, and Mom was keeping her home from school so she could take her to the doctor in Faulkton.

"What do you want, Susie?" I called from the kitchen.

"Would you come here . . . please?"

When I rolled my eyes, Dad saw me.

"For heaven's sake, go see what your little sister wants," he ordered.

I went to the room. "What do you want, Susie?"

"Would you go to my teacher and get my reading book for me, please?" she pleaded with soulful brown eyes. She was resting in bed.

"Sure. I hope you feel better when I get home," I told her, and I meant it.

Back in the kitchen, Kim and Carol were miffed about Mom's demand that we take our winter coats and overshoes.

Dad backed her up. "Listen to your mother. This weather feels like the calm before the storm."

*   *   *

It was a good thing we had those coats and overshoes!

By late morning, the temperature plummeted, and with the colder temperature came snow and wind. The school office heard the blizzard warnings after lunch. By the time news of the decision to dismiss school reached our classroom, snow was swirling in the air outside the windows. We stood up, our hinged seats swinging up as we did, and looked out the windows to see how bad it was.

"Winnie, we can't see your house!" David exclaimed. Her house was just half a mile across the open field and near the road.

"You can't see the baseball dugout, either!" cried Darren. That was about a third of the way to Winnie's house.

Here we go again! How many days of school will this blizzard force us to miss? I wondered. I started feeling sorry for my country-girl self and the possibility of snowbound days ahead on the farm. *Nothing ahead but shoveling snow and feeding cattle, feeding cattle and shoveling snow.*

Then I remembered Susie, and I worried about her being sick and maybe out in the snow — Mom and Matthew, too. *And Dad? Where is he? Is he going off to a sale today?*

The first five miles on the bus was like a trip into a snow

attack. The wind blew the wet flakes straight into the windshield, where they hit like blobs of splattered plaster. I wondered how Les could see well enough to keep the bus on the road.

When the route turned south on Highway 45, the wind caked the back of the bus with snow, too. Mr. Kahn was at the road again to walk Megan and Chip to their house. Joe Hart, who everyone called *Joie,* was at the road when David and Devon got off.

"How many more do you have to drop off?" Mr. Hart asked Les worriedly.

"Six. The Mackey kids and the Johnson girls," Les answered. "The rest were picked up at school."

"This snow is getting deeper by the minute," Mr. Hart said. "Do you think you can make it? Those extra two miles out to the Johnsons' and back could be tricky."

I don't like hearing that!

"I should be able to make it."

"Good luck to you. I'll call the Mackeys and let them know the kids are on the way. Too bad I can't call the Johnsons."

Because the Johnsons don't have a phone!

"Yup! I'd better get a move on!" Les said, eyeing the road

ahead. "Good! There's a snowplow heading this way. That'll help on the highway."

"But those county and township roads could be near impassable," Mr. Hart said. "If it looks like that's the case, turn around and come back here to wait out the storm." He waved to us as the bus passed by. Devon and David waved, too. They looked happy to be home. Their dad still looked worried.

The bus traveled a little faster once the snowplow passed. Thank goodness, we met only one car and one truck from the opposite direction, because we had to get off to the side in deeper snow. Both times, the bus wheels spun. Both times, I held my breath, fearing that we were stuck. Both times, I let out a sigh of relief as we drove forward.

When we turned onto the township road, going east, the only tracks were the deep ones that trailed *behind* us on the snow-covered road. That would make it harder to see the road between the ditches. Les must now forge ahead like a ship captain in the fog.

At the turnoff to the Mackeys', we lost momentum in a snowbank at the corner, and the bus stopped. Les attempted to get free by trying to drive forward and then backwards, but when the motor raced, the wheels just spun in place.

We're stuck!

Les made several attempts, shifting into forward and then reverse, but the bus only sank deeper into the snow. Finally he shook his head and turned off the motor.

We're stuck! We're really stuck! I didn't want to believe it. I looked around at the others' faces and saw disbelief in their eyes.

Les did not move at first. He must have been thinking about what to do. The six of us remaining in the bus sat as still as death. Then, slowly, Les rose from his seat. "I'm going to walk back to the highway," he said. "I'll find help and come back to get you."

He's going to leave us here alone? How is he *going to find his way?*

"Do not leave this bus and go wandering off!" Les commanded. "Stay here. You are safe here. You could get lost in a field out there if you leave. I *will* be back with someone to get you." He paused. "It may take a while, but I'll be back."

Per Hansa! I suddenly saw Les's face as that of the man sitting against the haystack with his skis beside him. But there were no haystacks between the bus and the Harts' place. And Les did not have skis for walking in the snow.

I tried to erase those thoughts from my mind, but I started thinking about the five North Dakota children who didn't make it home from school.

"Les?"

"Yes, Rachel."

"How will you find your way? How do we know *you* won't get lost in a field?"

"The bus tracks are still fresh and deep. I'll follow them back to the highway. There's bound to be a truck or car out on the road that will take me back to Joie's. *Stay in the bus!* You should be warm enough here until I get back."

For how long? I wanted to ask. Temperatures usually got very cold after a big snow.

"Close the door behind me, Dick!" Les instructed. Dick went to the front and stood behind the driver's seat. Les looked around at each of us. "I'll be back as soon as I can."

He swung the door handle forward, gave us a reassuring salute by his cap, then stepped down into the snow.

Dick closed the door behind him.

Chapter 7

Six faces, watching in silence from the bus windows, saw Les fade into the white of whirling snow.

When no sign of him was left, Kim asked, "How long do you think it will be before he comes back?"

"An hour," Dick said.

"If he doesn't get lost in the snow and freeze to death," I mumbled. *Like Per Hansa,* I thought.

"You worry too much, Rachel," Kim said.

"No I don't!"

In my mind, Les was our hope for survival. He was a good and kind man, like Per Hansa was. He would do his best, and he hadn't been forced to go against his better judgment as Per Hansa had been by his wife. That meant Les must have believed he could make it.

That thought made me feel a little better about our chances. But then I remembered the rest of my family.

Mom! Matthew! Susie! Dad! Not knowing their situations frightened me. *Please be home!*

When I heard Carol and Maureen talking softly about high school stuff, that comforted me a little. I, like most of us in the upper grades, was always interested in what the high school kids were up to.

Each of us had staked out a seat of our own, and Carol and Maureen had seats one behind the other. They sat with their backs against the windows and their legs stretched out on the seats. They didn't seem too worried, I noticed. They talked about who was dating whom.

"Dan gave Jenny his class ring to wear, so now they're going steady," Carol said about one of her friends who was dating a senior.

"His ring is so huge," Maureen replied. "Did you see how much tape Jenny had to wrap around it so it would fit?"

"Dan's a big guy." Carol laughed. "I think I'd wear it on a chain around my neck like Gretchen does with Bobby's ring."

"But then Gretchen has to wear it under her cheerleading sweater. Otherwise it would bounce up and hit her in the face when she jumps around," Maureen said. "So how do guys from the away team know that she is going steady if they don't see a boy's class ring on her left finger?"

"I don't think Bobby's too worried about it. He knows Gretchen is crazy about him." Carol giggled.

Their conversation made me wonder whether I would ever go steady someday. I doubted that I would, because I didn't plan to get married until after college. A lot of high school kids who went steady ended up getting married before they finished college. I knew that I definitely wanted to finish college and maybe go to New York City to study ballet.

There was a lull in their chatter, and my thoughts turned to home and everyone there. I fingered aimlessly in the fog that formed on the windows and tried to picture all of them safe and at home, hoping the electricity would stay on so they wouldn't be in the dark. I wrote RACHEL in the fog and then I wrote JOHNSON.

I eyed the foggy window next to mine.

"Hey, Carrie, want to play cat and mouse?" I asked, hoping to take my mind off Les and my family.

"Sure!" she said. Carrie was a fourth-grader and was sitting in the seat behind me.

I drew the two straight lines down and two straight lines across those to make nine spaces. "You go first!" I said.

Carrie placed an *X* in the center space. I fingered an *O* in the top right. Carrie filled in bottom right. I blocked her at top left. She marked middle right. I saw that it was going to be a draw.

"I start this time!" I said, and placed an *O* in top left. Carrie drew an *X* in the center space. I drew an *O* in bottom right. Carrie marked top right. *Good! I get three outside corners.* I marked bottom left. That three-corner strategy often worked for me. Carrie put an *X* in the center bottom. I fingered my *O* in center left and scratched the line down the left column of *O*s. "Gotcha!"

Within a few minutes, Carrie and I had used up the fog on the windows on our side of the bus like pages in a tablet. Kim and Dick, playing hangman, had used up the fog on the other side.

I erased the foggy windows on our side with my hand. The glass felt much colder than before. Then I noticed the chill in the bus.

Weariness settled over us. No one spoke for a few minutes, and the silence that hovered was depressing.

I wrapped my coat around me a little tighter and laid my head on my hands on the back of my seat. Carol's eyes caught mine, and she gave me a sympathetic smile.

"Hey, let's sing something," she said.

No one answered.

"I don't want to sing by myself!"

"I'll sing," Carrie said.

"Me, too," I said.

"Kim?" Carol asked.

"Oh sure," she agreed.

"What do you want to sing?" Carol asked.

"How about 'Comin' Round the Mountain'?" Carrie suggested.

"We can sing that one," Carol said. She started us off:

"She'll be coming round the mountain when she comes.
Toot! Toot!
She'll be coming round the mountain when she comes.
Toot! Toot!
She'll be coming round the mountain,

she'll be coming round the mountain,
she'll be coming round the mountain when she comes.
Toot! Toot!"

We raised an arm in the air and pulled the imaginary train whistle, the way we did when Mrs. Olson taught us this song in third and fourth-grades.

"She'll be driving six white horses when she comes!
Whoa back!"

Driving six white horses? She must come to town on the train and then switch to the horses, I thought.

Dick got into the spirit of the song. He added "*when she comes*" while we held the word *comes* for extra beats.

"We'll all go out to meet her when she comes. Hi, babe!"

At the end we sang all the sound words in reverse order: *Hi, babe! Whoa back! Toot! Toot!*

The next song was "Row, Row, Row Your Boat." Kim and Dick did the counter round, trying to make us have more fun. It had a good beat, like "Comin' Round the Mountain."

"Let's sing 'Way Down Upon the Swanee River,'" Maureen suggested.

"Sure," Carol said and started:

"Way down upon the Swanee River,
far, far away,
that's where my heart is turning ever,
that's where the old folks stay."

That song had some sad words in its chorus:

"All the world is sad and dreary,
everywhere I roam.
Oh, brother, how my heart grows weary,
far from the old folks at home."

It made me miss *my* folks at home. I could not block the image of Mom *also* stranded in a snowbank, in the car with Matthew and Susie. I pictured that worried furrow in her brow. I wondered if *she* was singing to my little brother and sister. I couldn't imagine Dad anywhere. I guess because I hadn't paid enough attention this morning to know where he was.

"We've fogged the windows again," Dick said.

"That's because there's a lot of hot air in here — mostly yours!" Kim teased.

Suddenly, with the windows fogged up, it seemed that the bus was closing in on me — like a prison. Quickly I wiped off a window so I could see outside, maybe even catch a glimpse of Les, but there was nothing but white. The moisture was cold on my hand, and the fog was starting to harden. White frost clung to the corners of the windows.

"What time is it?" I asked Carol.

She checked her wristwatch. "Three-thirty."

"Les's been gone over an hour," I said softly.

Chapter 8

We drew our coats and scarves more snugly around us.

Outside, the gray had grown a shade darker. The windows fogged over again and again. We wrote in the fog. Carrie practiced her new cursive strokes — ovals and diagonals — "to achieve flourish in one's penmanship."

We drew in the fog. I had discovered that a piece of hardening fog, not quite yet frost, could be moved around on the window.

When the fog turned to frost, we scratched our writing across it.

"What time is it now?" I asked Carol.

"Four o'clock," she answered softly.

"What can be keeping Les?" I wondered out loud.

Dick, who squirmed a little and then crossed his legs,

said, "The snow was deep and getting deeper. It's hard work and takes a long time to walk in deep snow."

"What if he gets tired and sits down?" Again I saw Per Hansa, sitting with his back against the haystack.

"Les is a strong man," Dick said. "I saw him in swim trunks once, and he has calf muscles this big." His two hands formed a big exaggerated circle and made everyone laugh. Even me, for a split second.

Still, it was getting dark, and Les had been gone for such a long time.

"What if he doesn't come back tonight?" I asked.

"We're not going to think that way," Carol declared. "Let's play a game. How about the guessing game? Everyone agree?"

We did, halfheartedly.

Dick was first to pick something for us to guess. He seemed nervous. He uncrossed his legs and crossed them the other way before picking an object and giving us a clue. "It's gray!"

"Rachel's jacket," Carrie said.

"Nope!"

"What size?" Kim asked.

"Small."

We all looked around for something small and gray. Kim didn't guess.

"What shape is it?" Carol asked.

"Irregular." Dick squirmed a little.

We looked around for something gray, small, and irregular.

"Can we see it?" Maureen asked.

"Nope."

"Can *you* see it?" Carrie asked.

"Yup!"

We all converged on his seat to see what he could see.

"The gray stuffing in the rip of the seat," Carrie said quickly so no one would say it before her.

"Yup!"

"That's not small!" Kim argued. "The stuffing covers the whole seat."

"But *I* can only see what's in the rip!" Dick wriggled and tensed his body. With those movements, I suspected what the matter was.

Within seconds he rose, clutching his crotch. "I can't hold it any longer!" he burst out. "I have to pee!" he cried, and ran for the door.

"Les said to stay in the bus," I reminded him.

"He didn't mean for this. He meant don't wander off. I'm not going to wet my pants and sit here in the cold! Maureen, come shut the door behind me. I'll stay right by the bus — the front of the bus — so *none* of you girls can *see* me." He continued clutching his crotch and wriggling until Maureen got to the door and opened it for him so he could keep his hands on diaper duty.

After Dick dashed out, Maureen shut the door quickly to keep out the cold; then she wiped a spot on the windshield. "I can only see the top of him," she said. "He'll be fine."

"It's a lot easier for him than it is for the rest of us," Kim complained.

"Don't tell me you have to go?" Carol exclaimed.

"No, not yet. But if we're here much longer . . ."

Suddenly we heard Dick yell. "Hey, girls! There's a light coming behind the bus!"

We raced to the back of the bus. Kim got there first and scratched through the frost on the back window. "It *is* a light! Someone's coming for us!"

"Someone's coming for us!" we yelled. I jumped up and down. Carrie did, too. Our jumping shook the bus.

A small round beacon shone through the blowing snow.

Someone was carrying a flashlight — not to find their way, but to let others see them coming. To let *us* see them coming.

"Hey, Les? That you?" Dick yelled. He had moved behind the bus.

Two shapes, one carrying the flashlight, emerged from the swirling gray. "Hello?" called one.

"That's Les's voice!" Carrie said.

The two were bundled in parkas, hoods tied closely around their faces, leaving only a small opening for their eyes and noses.

"Maureen, open the door!" Dick shouted, pounding on the door. "Les is here!"

Maureen opened the door, and along with the snow and the wind, in rushed Dick with Les and the other person. Les loosened his snowy hood before plunking into the driver's seat with his snow-laden parka. He was breathing hard.

When the second person pulled back his hood, we discovered with delight that it was Devon Hart.

"Devon! Our hero!" Carrie cried.

"Don't forget *Les!*" I reminded her. Carrie had a crush on Devon even though he was five years older.

"Les, too!" she added.

"We're not heroes until we all get back to the high-way, where Joie is waiting for us with his truck — and until we make it safely to his place," Les said. "Bundle your-selves as warm as you can. Cover your faces with a scarf, a collar, or at least your hands, because the wind takes your breath away!"

"I discovered that, taking a pee," muttered Dick.

Devon laughed.

"We can't waste any more time here," Les said. "It is hard to see, now that dusk is closing in. Just a bit of the bus tracks are showing, and we will lose that trail very soon in this wind," he warned. "Everyone must keep hold of some-one else's hand so we don't lose anyone. Carrie, you're pretty small, and the snow is getting deep — if you get tired, I'll carry you piggyback."

"I won't get tired!" Carrie declared.

"Okay, good." Les nodded. "I'll lead. Devon and Dick, you take up the rear. Between us, you girls hold on to some-one's hand."

"I don't have to hold hands with Devon, do I?" Dick joked.

Les was not in a mood for joking. "Keep track of each other. If the wind takes your breath away, you may have to stop. If the other person keeps on going — well, we could lose you. So stay close, everyone!" He glanced quickly at Carol.

"Carol, your glasses will be plastered immediately. It's best that you take them off in here." Then he asked, "Will you be able to see okay without them?"

"Yes," she answered, and took them off. "They're for distance vision, and we can't see very far tonight anyway." She folded them and put them in her big coat pocket.

"Devon, shut this door good when we're all out," Les said. He was the first one out, and he started leading our group. Maureen took Carrie's hand, and they walked behind Les. I was in the middle between Carol and Kim. Dick and Devon followed us.

The wind raged from the northwest, assaulting us with a direct onslaught of pelting snow in our faces as we headed west. I had to let go of Kim's hand so I could cover as much of my face as possible.

"Hang on to my coat, Kim, so you don't get separated from us," I said.

She gripped the opening flap of my pocket.

With each step, I sank in the snow higher than the tops of my overshoes.

Making headway was difficult, so Carol, Kim, and I tried walking backwards so the wind would hit our backs instead of our faces. But that was even harder and slower. Dick and Devon were soon on our toes, rather than our heels, and that slowed them down.

"Devon?" Les had turned around and walked backwards while calling; otherwise his words would have been stolen away by the wind. The flashlight beam at his side bounced in time to his steps.

"I'm here!"

"Just checking! Johnson girls?"

"We're here!" we answered, moving our hands, then quickly re-covering our faces.

"Maureen? Carrie?"

"Right here!"

"Good! We've got to keep going. Shouldn't be much farther." Les turned around, and the flashlight cast its beam on the ground ahead.

My legs were tiring. I was slowing down. Kim and Carol

seemed to be pulling me. Carrie was lagging a little behind Maureen, too.

Les turned to us and stopped. "Let's take a break . . . stop for a minute . . . give us a chance to catch our breath."

We huddled together. The rest was brief, for soon Les said, "Okay, let's not keep Joie waiting or he'll worry!"

We trudged on. *Les said it shouldn't be much farther.* I wondered just how far it really was.

I grasped Carol's hand tighter. Suddenly I realized that I didn't feel Kim's grip on my coat. *Kim? Where's Kim?* I swung my arm to the right, leaving my face open to the wind. It struck only air instead of Kim.

"Kim!" I hollered.

"I'm . . . coming," she answered breathlessly.

"Carol, slow down for Kim!"

"Okay. I've got your coat again, Rachel," Kim said.

I felt so tired. I wasn't sure how much farther I could go. I could hardly lift my foot out of the snow to take the next step.

I started thinking about Per Hansa again. *Was this how he felt before he stopped to rest against the haystack?*

Chapter 9

"There it is! There's the truck!" Les shouted. "Thank God we've made it this far!"

We're not lost! We're not lost! I had been so absorbed in Per Hansa's story that it was hard to tell what was real anymore. Was the stuck bus real or a dream? Was this rescue real or a dream?

"Man, am I glad to see you!" Mr. Hart said when we reached the truck. "I was beginning to worry. Everyone okay?" He lifted an earflap on his gray cap to hear the reply.

"We're here!" Les said. "There might be a few weary leg muscles, but we're here. What a bunch of troopers they are, too, I tell you. How many can we squeeze in the cab?"

Mr. Hart pondered. "Five girls. That'd be a tight squeeze."

"I'll ride in the back," I said.

"Me, too," Kim said.

"Carrie can sit on my lap," Maureen volunteered.

"Okay! Carol, Maureen, Carrie, in the cab. The rest of us in back," Les ordered.

Dick and Devon were already in the back of the small livestock truck. The top racks were folded down, so the truck was probably last used to haul sheep or hogs to market. Most likely Mr. Hart had cleaned it out, just as Dad cleaned his truck after hauling livestock. If not, there was plenty of snow on the box floor to cover any manure.

Kim and I climbed in, and Les followed. Sitting on the floor of the box offered some protection from the raging wind, but the snow swirled above us and through the air slats. There was a slat removed, and it allowed me to see through the cab's back window and out the windshield between Carol's and Maureen's heads. Wind blew snow against the windshield. When the wind eased, I saw that the plowed lane was not very wide, and sweeping drifts lay across the road.

Mr. Hart headed north to his farm one mile ahead. The snow was, as Dad would say, hell-bent southward, thwarting Mr. Hart's progress.

Dad? Mom? Matthew? Susie? Are they *safe?*

Their names moved through my mind in rhythm with the wipers as I watched them labor to clean the snow from the windshield. The wipers swept across the glass, clearing the snow to the sides. But the snow, as if playing a dirty trick on the wipers, coated the windshield before they could sweep back. Then the snow packed together at the bottom of the windshield and along the sides with each sweep. That made the vision area grow smaller.

Strong gusts forced Mr. Hart to stop the truck now and then. He would jump out of the cab, clear the snow from the windshield, and then climb back in and drive forward. When the truck's wheels spun in one large drift, I thought, *We're not safe yet, and it's getting dark. We could get stranded on* this *road!*

More drifts threatened our progress. We must have been traveling the longest mile in the world. Then I noticed that the people in the cab were pointing at something. Soon I saw it, too: the shape of a sign by the road — the sign that I knew read REGISTERED POLLED HEREFORDS. JOE HART & SONS.

"We're at the farm!" I shouted, then backed away from the slat so the others could see.

The truck turned into the farmyard and stopped at the gate near the house. The five of us in back scrambled over the top of the box rack and jumped down. We brushed the snow from our coats and scarves and caps.

"Devon," Mr. Hart called to his son, "tell your mother we're going to put the truck in the shed and check the cattle in the barn before we come in."

David, who was shoveling the snow on the sidewalk, opened the gate to the house for us.

"Hi, Rachel!" he said.

"Hi, David. Awful snowstorm."

"Ah, it's not so bad — get to miss school tomorrow."

"And probably a few more days after that," I replied with a roll of my eyes.

Devon led us to the house and into the porch just off the kitchen.

"Devon, I'm so glad to see you!" Mrs. Hart exclaimed.

"Mom, I have to run help Dad put the truck away and check the cattle in the barn."

"Okay, dear. You and your dad be careful. It's getting dark."

"We can see the yard light, Mom," he said before dashing out.

"Hello, everyone! Come in!" Mrs. Hart welcomed us. "You must be frozen! Hang up your wraps and come in. Les, you must be exhausted after all that walking in the snow."

"I am grateful to be here with all the kids," Les said, "thanks to you and Joie."

"I'm glad you're all here, too. I'd rather the kids were safe at their own homes, but it wasn't to be." She smiled sympathetically at Les and then asked, "Did everyone find hooks for their coats?"

We had. Some of us doubled up on hooks. It wasn't until I took off my jacket that I realized how cold I was.

"Goodness, Rachel, you're shivering," Mrs. Hart said. "And Carrie, too! Come in the living room and stand by the fireplace, but not too close. I don't want you to catch on fire."

The fireplace was a gas stove shaped like a big half log on its side, with white tile pieces behind a grill. The tile became a glowing red when the gas-fired flames were burning. It warmed our hands and faces quickly; then we turned, and the heat felt good on our backs.

"I can only imagine how worried your parents must be," Mrs. Hart said. "I talked to the Mackeys on the phone earlier, so they would know Les and Joie were bringing you here. I also called them when I saw the truck drive in. They know you are safe. But my dear Johnson girls"— she shook her head —"you still haven't convinced your dad to get a phone put in, huh?"

"He's obstinate on that subject," Carol said.

"Well, my heart goes out to your parents. How hard it must be for them, not knowing if you are safe!"

"Or for us to know if *they* are safe," I added. *If we could call home, this wouldn't be a problem.*

"Yes, I guess it works both ways at a time like this," she said. "Oh, let's hear what the radio has to say." She walked to the kitchen and turned up the volume on the radio.

"There will be no school tomorrow in any of the Faulk County schools," the male announcer said. "That includes rural and town schools. All basketball games and after-school activities have also been canceled or postponed until further notice. There will be no pancake supper at Our Savior Lutheran Church in Faulkton this evening. The Cresbard School Board meeting scheduled for tonight has been postponed. The Scatterwood Community Club Square Dance has been canceled for tomorrow night. The Seneca

4-H Club has canceled its meeting for tomorrow night. We will update you on all cancellations as we receive them. Now for the weather report . . ."

Suddenly Mrs. Hart's face brightened. "The radio! I'll call the radio and ask them to announce that the Tony Johnson girls on Les Arnsee's Cresbard bus are safe at the Joe Hart farm. They'll surely be listening to the radio."

"If . . . they're home, Mrs. Hart," I said softly.

"*If* they're home?"

"Mom was going to take Susie to the doctor today. And Dad might have gone to a sale."

"Rachel, they're probably home and just fine," Kim said. "You worry too much."

"No I don't!"

Mrs. Hart gave me a sympathetic smile. "I'll call the radio station now," she said, and returned to the kitchen. She turned the radio down to make the call. We listened to her request the announcement. She included the Mackey children.

"There. They'll announce it soon and repeat it every hour until ten p.m. and then again in the morning." She turned up the radio volume again.

". . . People are urged to have emergency power measures handy and prepare for a possible power outage as a result of this storm. Twelve inches of wet snow have already fallen on the ground in Faulk County. Presently, high winds are gusting to fifty miles per hour. The snow and wind are expected to continue through the night, with temperatures falling near or below zero. At least twelve more inches of snow are expected tonight . . ."

Power outage? If the power goes off, Mom and Dad won't hear the announcement at home. Mom will be frantic. On the other hand, if they are in the car or the truck and they have the radio on, they'll hear. They could be buried in snow by morning, but at least they'll know we are safe. No comfort in that! It's merely a twist on Per Hansa's ending.

Why, oh why, don't we have a phone?

Chapter 10

At suppertime we heard the announcement.

"The children on Les Arnsee's Cresbard school bus are safe at the home of Joe Hart . . ."

"There it is!" Kim exclaimed.

"Shhh! There's more!" Carol ordered.

". . . That includes the Ronald Mackey children and the Tony Johnson children. Again — the Ronald Mackey and Tony Johnson children are safe at the Joe Hart home."

Several sighs of relief were heard around the table.

"I'm sure your parents will feel enormous relief after that announcement," Mrs. Hart said. When she smiled at me, I tried to return a weak smile, for she was very sweet.

Maybe Mom and Dad did hear it.

It was the women's turn at the table. The men and boys had eaten first and were relaxing in the living room. Mrs. Hart's supper was similar to one that Mom often made at uncertain times — pancakes and sausage patties. There was homemade applesauce with a pink tinge from the ripe peels that probably had been strained in the final step before canning.

Maureen, Carol, and Kim helped Mrs. Hart clear the table and wash and wipe the dishes. Carrie and I went into the living room, where the others were watching moving pictures on the front of a small boxlike apparatus they called a television.

Oh, my! It was like a tiny picture show that we would sometimes see on weekends in the theater at Cresbard or Faulkton. *A picture show in their own house!*

I knew that a lot of people had them in their homes. Winnie and Melissa did. On one trip to the nearby city of Aberdeen, Mom and Dad had checked them out in the Sears department store. Dad had not been impressed.

"I think this television thing could just be a fad," he had declared that night at the dinner table. "Anyway, I'm not interested in having one until the reception is better. There's too much static, and the picture is too snowy. Me? I prefer a radio," he added.

Carrie and I had walked into the Harts' living room just as a program called *I Love Lucy* was starting. Music played while the words *I LOVE LUCY* . . . STARRING LUCILLE BALL AND DESI ARNAZ wrote themselves across the screen behind what looked like snow falling. Static made the sound fuzzy sometimes. Not clear like a radio's. I understood my dad's reaction to the quality of the picture and sound.

But it wasn't long after I sat down that I was caught up, along with the others, in the crazy antics of Lucy. It made me forget my troubles, and I stopped worrying about my family for a while.

When it was time to go to bed, I thought, *That was fun. I hope the picture and sound improve, and then we can have one, too.*

Carol, Kim, and I were assigned to the guest bedroom off the living room. David, Devon, and Dick slept in one of the bedrooms upstairs, Maureen and Carrie in the other. A bed was prepared for Les on the couch, and Mr. and Mrs. Hart had their own bedroom off the kitchen.

Before falling asleep, I prayed, *Please let Mom and Dad, Susie, and Matthew be okay at home!*

*   *   *

I woke to a bright room. At the sight of unfamiliar pink walls, the memory of yesterday's storm flooded back, and so did the fears of yesterday. Since the room was so bright, I was sure the snow must have stopped. I sat up to look out the window and saw that it had.

Outside the window, white snow stretched to the horizon — all was white except for the power-line poles and the very tops of the fence posts along the highway.

Having no pajamas, I had slept in my undershirt and underpants. I carefully crawled out of my middle spot in the bed. I didn't want to wake Carol or Kim. I brushed my hair with the brush that Mrs. Hart had put in our room for us. After all, there were boys in this house. Then I quickly put on my dress and shoes and socks and sought the comfort of the voices in the kitchen.

I recognized the radio announcer's voice. The Harts were listening to the same country news program that Mom and Dad listened to in the mornings.

"Good morning, young lady," Mr. Hart said. "I hope you slept well."

"I did," I replied, surprised that I had slept at all.

On the radio, Eddy Arnold started singing "Cattle Call."

It was a catchy tune about a cowboy herding his cattle while singing *"his lonesome cattle call."* After those words, Eddy Arnold would yodel. I guess that was the cattle call. It reminded me of Dad's yodeling when he worked during the night out on a tractor. His *yodel ladle lee* and other nonsense syllables would sound across the fields in the night air, all the way to home. Yodels. That's all he sang. No words. It was a lovely song.

"Good morning, Rachel," Mrs. Hart said, bringing me back to the present. She was busy at the stove.

"Morning, Mrs. Hart."

Suddenly snow flew across the outside of the porch window, which I could see from the kitchen. I glimpsed Dick and Devon shoveling a narrow path on the sidewalk to the house. The snow was up to their waists.

"There's a lot of snow to shovel out there!" I exclaimed.

"We fed them a good breakfast first." Mr. Hart chuckled. "We're eating in shifts this morning. Are you ready for your breakfast?"

"Sure!" I replied. "The eggs and bacon smell great, Mrs. Hart." I turned to Mr. Hart. "Do I have to shovel snow?"

"Nah! We don't have that many shovels. We'll let the boys do it."

"I'd have to help at home. We don't have any big boys, just our baby brother."

I fell quiet, and so did they. They knew my thoughts.

Mrs. Hart broke the silence. "How many eggs and slices of bacon, Rachel?"

"One egg, two slices of bacon," I answered. I thanked her when she set the plate at my place.

Eddy Arnold yodeled his last cattle call, and the announcer said, "Next the weather, road conditions, and cancellations. Stay tuned following this message."

The message was a commercial proclaiming the wonders of Brylcreem, a hair product for men. The commercial ended with its musical jingle, *"Brylcreem! A little dab'll do ya!"*

The announcer continued: "The snow has ended for today. Twenty-six inches fell in the last eighteen hours. Last night's low temperature was fourteen degrees. Today it will be sunny, with a high near twenty-five degrees, winds out of the northwest about five to ten miles per hour. There will be no school today at any of the Faulk County schools *and* until further notice. No school at Faulk County schools today and until further notice."

Had I been at home, I would have groaned at the announcement. I knew that at home I would be shoveling snow and feeding cattle. Here at the Harts', they had all kinds of boys to do the hard work. And here, there were other kids besides my siblings to do stuff with.

This is like a vacation! And if we had a phone and my parents knew we were safe and I knew that they were safe, I could really enjoy myself. Worrying about Mom and Dad puts a damper on my fun.

"Now for the road reports: the county road department reports that most roads are impassable. The snowplows were called off the roads last night due to the high winds, drifting snow shutting the roads behind the plows. All snowplows are back out this morning and will be working around the clock. The sheriff requests that residents stay off the roads until further notice. If an emergency arises, contact the sheriff's office."

Mr. Hart's face lit up when the announcer continued: "We have been notified that all of the children on the Cresbard school bus driven by Les Arnsee are safe at the Joe Hart home. That includes the Ronald Mackey children and the Tony Johnson children."

When the announcer finished, Mr. Hart broke in immediately. "By George! Why didn't I think of this earlier?" He pounded his fist lightly on the table. "I'll call the sheriff's office and see if they have any information on missing or stranded people."

"I don't know that that's such a good idea, Joie," Mrs. Hart cautioned. She gave her head a slight jerk in my direction, as if to remind him that I was present.

She doesn't want me to hear this in case there's bad news. But it could be good news, and then I wouldn't have to worry about them.

But Mr. Hart was already dialing the phone. He asked for information on Tony Johnson and Leona Johnson, giving possible locations in separate vehicles in different directions from their home.

"Nothing on him, then?" He glanced at me, then waited. "Nothing on her, either? . . . Any airplanes out searching for stranded people? . . . Later this morning! . . . Yup! It's their girls that are here with us. . . . We'd appreciate it . . . Okay . . . Thanks! Bye!"

"No news is good news in this case, wouldn't you say, Vi?" Mr. Hart asked his wife.

"I have a good feeling after that call, Rachel, that your parents *are* home," Mrs. Hart said.

I attempted a smile. I was not convinced, but I felt a little better.

Chapter 11

Mr. Hart removed snow from the yard and doorways of the barn, shed, and garage the whole day through. Devon, David, and Dick used shovels to move the snow from difficult spots to paths where Mr. Hart's hydraulic farmhand could gather and remove it to piles. The farmhand attached to the tractor collected large amounts of the white stuff in its scoop, and with the pull or push of a lever, the snow was raised into the air and dumped on a gleaming pile.

The mounds of cold powder mixed with frozen chunks grew higher and, at the end of the day, stood like sentinels around the yard.

The next morning, I felt restless. I wasn't used to sitting around the house and doing so little. *I have to get out and get some exercise. These walls are hemming me in.*

"Carrie, want to go outside?" I asked.

"Brrrr," she replied, shaking her head. She was content reading one of David's Superman comic books.

I bundled up for maximum warmth, grateful for a pair of David's denim jeans that Mrs. Hart had lent me. I ventured outside and walked through the maze of snow piles. Yesterday they looked like they were guarding the yard in a serious way. Today they seemed to invite play.

"Hey, Rachel?" David yelled from the barn. "I'm done with chores. Want to have some fun?"

"That depends on what it is."

"Sliding down these mounds!"

"Yeah, sure!" I was game.

"Let's try this one here." He pointed to one outside the barnyard.

As we climbed to the top of the mound, chunks of snow tumbled down. Once we finally reached the peak, the only things above us were the barn and the black T crossbeams on top of the power poles.

Beneath the cloudless, perfect blue sky stretched an endless plain of white fields, interrupted in only a few spots by neighboring farms and the windbreak groves that were planted to stop or slow the speed of the almost constant

South Dakota winds. The several rows of trees, often reaching a quarter to a half mile, offered protection to livestock and crops.

"Maybe I can see our farm from up here," I said.

"Nope, can't see it," David said. I nodded. I saw the reason: a grove of trees — *our own windbreak trees* — on a rise a few miles to the southeast blocked the farm from view.

"I hope my family's okay." I allowed my gaze to linger in that direction.

"I hope so, too," David said. "Ready?" he added.

"You first! Push those chunks out of the way for me." I laughed.

David chose the smoothest side to slide down, feet first on his seat. His ride was choppy, but he had cleared the run of chunks for the next slide down.

"Okay, your turn!" he called up to me.

I sat down at the peak, feet first, and gave myself a little shove with my hands. "That was fun!" I exclaimed at the bottom.

"Once we get the sliderun smoother, it'll be faster," David said. He was already halfway up the pile, and I followed.

He was right. The next slide down was faster, and my stomach tickled in delight. We scrambled back up the pile and slid down again several times. Each time, the slide was faster and the sensation more intense. David's borrowed denim jeans were a godsend. My corduroy jeans would have been worn through the cloth in no time.

In our glee, we had failed to notice all the snow that had scattered around the bottom from our climbs and slides.

But Mr. Hart noticed.

"That's enough of that!" His booming voice came from the barn doorway. "We don't want that snow back on the yard, you two!"

David and I looked sheepishly at each other with raised eyebrows.

"Looked like fun, though," Mr. Hart admitted.

"Hey, Dad, can we go check on Devon and Dick up at the other barn?"

"Yeah, but they should be about done feeding the cattle there."

"How about it? Want to go?" David asked me.

"Sure!" The idea of walking that quarter mile gave me a sense of freedom after being housebound for a day.

We took the road — had it all to ourselves. A snowplow had not been through since the storm, so there was no traffic. The only signs of other human beings were the deep tracks left by Devon and Dick as they had headed toward the barn. David and I tried to step in their footprints, but the boys were bigger and heavier than we were, and their tracks were too deep. We found it easier to make our own path, because we sank only up to our calves. Halfway there, we stopped to catch our breath.

"Burma-Shave!" I laughed at the small advertising signs on the fence posts that peeked out from the deep snow. "'Within this . . . world of sin . . .'" I read from the second and third signs.

"'Your head . . . grows bald . . .'" David joined in with numbers four and five. "'But not . . . your chin!'" We laughed.

"Burma-Shave!" we shouted together.

"The Lord only knows how many times we've read those signs while driving by in the bus!" I said.

"Or me, driving by on the tractor or riding in the car every day," David added. "I think I've rested enough to move on. You ready?"

"I can breathe again without gasping, so let's get going."

We continued the tedious trek and were short of breath again when we reached the barn.

Near the barn, reddish-brown white-faced Herefords ate baled hay that had been tossed from the haymow door. Other cattle were lined up along both sides of a feeding bunk, eating ground corn.

"There isn't much hay out here." David pondered. "Considering the time Devon and Dick have been feeding them."

"I don't hear anyone," I said. "There should be sounds of *some* kind."

"Devon? Dick?" David hollered as he approached the haymow door.

No answer.

"Devon? Dick?" Louder this time.

No answer.

"This is strange," David said. "Let's go inside." I followed him into the barn. There was no sign of anyone. He looked around the different partitions and in the grain bin section. No one.

"Maybe they're up in the haymow," I suggested.

David climbed the wooden-slat ladder built up the side of the wall. A square hole cut into the floor above the ladder was the opening to the haymow inside the barn. When

I emerged through the door in the floor, the smell of dry alfalfa filled the air. When my eyes adjusted to the haymow's dim light, I saw layers of square bales tied with twine and stacked in neat rows. Off to one side, there was a pile of several bales that looked like they may have tumbled off the top. There was no sign of the two boys.

"Where could they be?" I asked.

"Are you guys hiding on us?" David yelled, then stopped to listen for an answer. Muffled cattle footsteps and cows chomping were the only sounds. "Come on, you guys, where are you?" There was a note of fear in his voice.

"Let's check for tracks leading away from the barn," I said, pointing to a small closed door in the wall. David unlatched it and swung it outward. We examined the snow around the barn. There was no sign of Devon or Dick.

David began walking the perimeter of the haymow to see if they were hiding behind or between the bales. I climbed to the top of the stacked bales of hay to survey the situation from that point.

"David," I whispered. "Stop! Listen! I thought I heard something!"

He stopped, and we stood listening. The sounds of the cows seemed loud.

"I don't hear anything," David whispered.

"There! There it is again."

A faint "Nnnn . . . help!" came from the tumbled pile of bales. The sound came again. "Oooooh . . . we need help!"

Frightened, David and I moved toward the sound.

The moans continued. "Mmmm . . . uuhh." They were coming from beneath the pile.

"That's Devon!" David started tossing bales away from the moans. I helped. My heart raced for fear at what we might find.

Sprawled inside the heap were Devon and Dick, emitting guttural moans. We were horrified.

"What happened?" I pleaded.

"Devon, what's the matter?" David implored.

"A . . . tramp . . . uuuh," Devon moaned.

Dick joined the moaning. "A tramp . . . beat . . . us . . . up. We . . . can't . . . move."

"Where is he?" David was frantic.

"Don't . . . know. Run . . . home . . . get . . . help!" Devon groaned.

"Is the tramp still here?" My heart was throbbing.

"Go . . . home . . . need help," Devon repeated.

"We can't just leave them like this!" I exclaimed.

"Don't . . . stay here. You . . . both . . . must go . . . He might . . . still . . . be here."

"Devon, I can't leave you here!" David declared.

"Go . . . now!" he ordered.

"You're sure?"

"Yes . . . go . . . both . . . go!"

"Okay, Devon! We'll be back with help as soon as we can!" David promised his brother.

Down the ladder we sped, back across the field and up the road we trudged.

"David, do you think . . . the tramp's . . . watching us?" I gasped for breath.

"Hard telling."

"They sounded . . . bad."

"Yeah."

"Why would a tramp be out in this weather? Do you think he's hiding from the sheriff?" I asked.

"Tramps usually come around this area in the summer. Maybe whoever it is . . . stayed around later this year . . . took shelter in the barn when he saw the bad weather coming."

We stopped talking and concentrated our energy on tromping through the snow.

Close to his home, David saw his father in the yard. "Dad!" he yelled. "Devon . . . Dick . . . have been beaten up . . . by a tramp!"

"Hurry! Help them . . . they might be dying." I was out of breath, perspiring, and my legs were weak.

"What's that you say about a tramp?" Mr. Hart asked when we reached him.

"Devon and Dick . . . are buried in some bales. They said . . . the tramp beat them up!" David reported.

"They . . . could hardly . . . talk," I said.

Mr. Hart looked quizzically at us, and then his gaze moved up the road to the barn.

He squinted against the midday sun. "You say they're buried in bales?" he asked, a slight smile crossing his face.

"Yeah!" We both nodded emphatically.

"They don't look buried to me!" Mr. Hart laughed and pointed toward the barn.

Devon and Dick were walking toward the farm, laughing and waving at us.

Chapter 12

Watching Devon and Dick whoop and congratulate themselves as they trudged toward the yard angered David and me.

"Devon, just you wait! I'm going to get so even with you!"

"Me, too! I think — I think I hate you! Both of you!" I shouted at them. My fists were clenched, I was that furious.

"Hey, Dick, are they mad or what?" Devon laughed as he sidestepped David's punch to his upper arm.

"I think they have good reason to be mad," Mr. Hart said. "That was a dirty trick you pulled on them. They ran for dear life to get help. You should have seen how out of breath they were. And their legs were weak and shaking."

"We know. We watched them run after they left the barn," Devon said, trying to control his laughter. When he looked at Dick and saw his quivering mouth muscles as *he* attempted to stifle *his* laughter, Devon broke up. Then Dick lost control, and both boys burst into boisterous belly laughter.

"We're just sorry . . . that we couldn't see the fright . . . on their faces as they were running. *'We can't just leave them like this!'* she said." Dick pointed at me as he mimicked me.

"*'Devon, I can't leave you here!'*" Devon mimicked David.

The laughter became infectious, and soon Mr. Hart was chuckling. Eventually, even David and I managed a smile — because in truth, we were glad that Devon and Dick were alive and we didn't have to worry about a tramp.

Even so, David took another quick punch at Devon's arm and landed a good one on him. Devon flinched, but faked toughness by putting his shoulder within David's reach and saying, "Go ahead, punch it if it'll make you feel better. It doesn't hurt, anyway."

David took a couple more punches before Mr. Hart put a stop to it. "That's enough, boys! Go into the house and wash up. Your mother and the girls have dinner about ready."

Kim was pouring milk into the glasses set at everyone's place. Carol pressed a few more strokes into the potatoes with the potato masher to mix the butter and milk thoroughly into them. The browned beef roast sat on a large platter near Mr. Hart. Maureen stirred the gravy, which was being made from the beef drippings in the roasting pan on the burner, so it wouldn't stick to the bottom of the pan. Then Mrs. Hart took the pan, poured the gravy into the gravy boat, and set it next to the large bowl of potatoes on the table.

I knew this signaled the end of dinner preparations. I had seen Mom do this so many times at home. Homesickness and fear seeped into my thoughts.

Are they home? Please, let them be home! If they are, I wonder what they're *eating. Do they know we are at the Harts'?*

My mind filled with contradictory images. In one, the rest of my family were safe at home around the table and aware that we were at the Harts'. In the other, they were stranded in snowbanks far from home. I blocked any further images from my mind.

"Rachel!" Kim nudged me with her elbow to take the bowl of potatoes she was passing to me. Next came the gravy boat. Mr. Hart had carved much of the roast, and that platter was right behind the gravy boat. Completing the supper was a bowl of green beans from a Mason canning jar, and an orange Jell-O salad made with shredded carrots from carrots that had been stored in a tub of sand in the Harts' cellar. I passed the Jell-O salad to Carrie and looked at all the good things on my plate. I had taken a little bit of everything, and the food smelled so good.

Mr. Hart had assigned Devon and David seats away from each other at the table. He knew David would have liked to take another punch or two at Devon. A couple of times, Devon and Dick had telltale smiles on their faces when they looked at David or me. David made faces at them. I was too worried about matters at home to react.

Most of the food on the table was eaten. It was good, but I knew it would have tasted even better if I were not so fearful about Mom and Dad. The conversation centered on the storm, the depth of the snow, and the results of calls to neighbors to check on how everyone was doing.

That night, Les wasn't at the supper table with us. He had walked a couple of miles up the road to bunk with the Kahns, since there were so many of us here at the Harts'. With only small children at that farm, Les could help them shovel out.

The only neighbors unaccounted for are my parents! If only we had a phone!

Then it dawned on me that if they weren't home, they wouldn't answer, and I would really be scared. This way, there was a fifty-fifty chance.

"It's time for the news," Mr. Hart said at six o'clock. Everyone quieted down to listen to the radio.

"And now for the local news. First, the weather: sunny skies covered the whole listening area today. The high temperature reached twenty-six degrees. A low of zero is expected tonight, with clear skies and wind speeds of five to ten miles per hour."

"Low winds," Mr. Hart interjected softly. "That's good."

"Tomorrow will be cloudy, with a fifty percent chance of snow flurries, high near twenty degrees, calm winds expected again tomorrow."

"Good!" Mr. Hart said. "If the winds stay low, snow shouldn't drift across the roads and block them — for at least a day, anyway. I certainly hope they're right about just flurries. Did you know, Vi," he continued, "that the plows made it pretty close to us today? We should be dug out by tomorrow morning."

"Good," she said, and sighed. Then she held her hand up for quiet so she could hear the next announcement.

"Highway 45 has one lane plowed from Faulkton to within a quarter mile of the Joe Hart farm. Coming from the north, Highway 45 has one lane open to the Highway 20 turnoff to Cresbard. We will return with more announcements after this message."

During the advertisement Mr. Hart said, "The snow is so deep that you can't see the snowplow after it clears the lane. The banks are higher than the plow. All you can see is the snow shooting over the top of the banks."

"Will cars have to wait to travel before two lanes are open?" David asked.

"Actually, the plow drivers will hollow out a space every so many yards for oncoming vehicles to park while they wait for another vehicle to pass. Plus, there are the driveways into farms that have been plowed. Vehicles can wait in those, too," Mr. Hart explained.

"It's going to be a *long* time before this snow is gone, isn't it?" Mrs. Hart said.

"It is January," Mr. Hart replied. "There's a lot of winter left." He paused, and then a smile crossed his face. "Remember before there were good snowplows and we had to shovel the roads out by hand? Remember that, Vi? When you were young?"

"Well, *I* never had to do it, but my father and brothers did," she said.

Talk of the old days reminded me of how much I enjoyed it when older folks came to dinner at our place and Mom and Dad would visit with them into the night. Dad, especially — because he was eight years older than Mom — had some interesting stories to tell from the old days. When he was a kid in West River, South Dakota, they had to walk along the railroad tracks in winter and pick up coal that dropped from the trains to burn in their stove. There were hardly any trees in that part of the state, so there wasn't any wood to burn. "Some corncobs, but in a bad year, those were few," he used to say.

When I compared Dad's memory to Mr. Hart's, my underlying fear resurfaced: *Are they okay . . .*

". . . All schools in Faulk County are canceled until further notice. All basketball games and extracurricular activities are canceled until further notice. Rural mail delivery has been suspended until further notice."

I waited for the bulletin about us being safe at the Harts', but the announcer concluded,

"That's the news for six o'clock, folks. Tune in again at ten o'clock for the latest updates."

"They didn't mention that we were safe!" I couldn't hide the alarm in my voice. "Why isn't the sheriff calling back with a report on Mom and Dad? Is it so bad that they don't want to devastate us in the middle of all this?"

No one offered any answers, but in the silence that followed, I felt everyone's sympathy.

Chapter 13

"Good morning, Claire!" Mr. Hart said into the telephone on our fifth day at the Harts'. He was talking to Claire Mackey, who was Carrie, Maureen, and Dick's uncle. He lived along the highway a couple of miles up. "By golly, you don't say! . . . He's coming through? . . . Does he have chains on? . . . I know that'll be good news to his girls!"

When the phone rang, I had stopped wiping the plates from breakfast. Every time the phone rang, no matter where I was in the house, I tuned in, hoping that it would be news about Mom or Dad. Kim was helping with dishes, too, and we looked at each other in anticipation of good news.

"Dad!" I whispered. She nodded.

"Yes, we'll tell the girls to get ready . . . About twenty

minutes yet? . . . Thanks, Claire!" Mr. Hart hung up the phone and turned to us with a smile.

"Was that about Dad? He made it home?" I asked. "Mom's okay, too?"

"Yup, they're fine. Your dad's coming with a tractor. He managed to get the tractor through the section road to Claire's, and they thought it would take about twenty minutes to get here from there. I think it could take longer, though," Mr. Hart said. "He asked that you be ready so he can head back right away."

"They heard the radio announcement?" I asked.

"Yup, the first time it went out."

"Praise God, they're all okay!" Mrs. Hart said.

"Yes. Both of them, and their two young ones are fine, too."

Tears of relief started to well up in my eyes. *Stop it, Rachel! Only babies cry!* I was able to blink them away before they rolled down my cheeks.

"I'll finish wiping the dishes, girls, so you can get ready." Mrs. Hart took the dishtowel from me. "Don't forget to use the bathroom before you go. That tractor ride will be cold, and it'll be a while before you get home."

I hurried off to the bathroom and to get my stuff together. I passed Carol playing Scrabble with Maureen in the living room. Evidently she had not heard the phone call.

"Carol, Dad will be here in about twenty minutes!" I said.

"Dad's coming?" she asked in surprise. "Then everyone's okay?"

"Yes. They were all at home."

"Thank heaven!"

"Now get ready to ride the *tractor* home!" Kim announced, watching, waiting for Carol's reaction.

"The tractor? We'll freeze to death!" Carol cried.

A wide grin spread across Kim's face. "Yeah! The tractor!" she said. "And Dad wanted us ready in twenty minutes, which was five minutes ago."

"Fifteen minutes. Heaven!"

"If Dad said he wanted us ready, he wants us ready," I pointed out. "Use the bathroom first," I reminded her.

"Who made you mother?" Kim snapped.

I narrowed my eyes and gave her a dirty look.

"Stop that, you two!" Carol ordered. "You'll make Mom and Dad real proud with that nonsense!"

"I'll go help Mrs. Hart with the dishes," Maureen said, excusing herself.

Carol, Kim, and I headed for the bathroom and bedroom, but first I stopped by a south window to look for the tractor. I stretched as tall as I could to see over the snowbanks, but I couldn't see over those high white walls along the road. I stretched once more and still didn't catch a glimpse. I would have to wait for a sight of Dad until he drove into the yard.

I hurried to the bedroom and took off the jeans that Mrs. Hart had lent me and laid them on the bed. I put on my dress and tucked it into my corduroy pants to keep the cold air out while on the tractor, and then I put on my sweater.

Part of me was sad to leave. When I hadn't been worrying about Mom and Dad, I had had a lot of fun — sliding down the mounds with David, the contrived adventure of the dangerous tramp, the conversations around the table, watching television, playing cards and games. And I didn't have to shovel any snow.

When all of the clothes I came with in the snowstorm were back on, I headed for the porch off the kitchen to put on my coat and scarf.

"Why don't you wait until your dad gets here?" Mrs. Hart suggested. "That way you won't get too hot before going out into the cold."

"Okay. I'll wait and watch from the living room window." Looking out toward the driveway, I could see that Mr. Hart must have used his hydraulic farmhand to clean up the messy snow that David and I had scattered around the bottom of the mound. The sides were smooth again, and there was a clear path in front of it.

In a few minutes I saw the nose of Dad's red tractor emerge between two white cliffs where the Harts' drive formed a T intersection with the highway.

"Here he is!" I exclaimed. I watched until the whole tractor and Dad came into view and turned into the drive. A greenish-brown canvas, called a comforter, with a clear plastic windshield was secured around the top and sides of the tractor engine. This shield blocked the wind and directed some of the engine heat back toward the driver. I could see Dad's face through the windshield. Chains were on the big rear tires.

I dashed into the kitchen and out to the porch for my coat and overshoes. Kim and Carol followed. Mr. Hart put down his cup of coffee and went to the outer porch door. He yelled out the door to Dad.

"Come on in, Tony! They're getting their coats on."

Dad stepped inside the porch, pulled down the hood of

his parka, and took off his thick sheepskin-lined glove before he shook hands with Mr. Hart.

Dad wasn't a hugging kind of person, so neither Carol, Kim, nor I rushed to hug him. He'd probably be embarrassed. Although Susie would have, and he would have been okay with it.

"Hi, Dad!" we said.

"Hi, girls! It looks like Mrs. Hart has taken good care of you," he said, smiling as he surveyed us.

We nodded. I could see in his eyes that he was happy to see us.

"Dad, how's Susie?" I was eager to know. "Did the doctor say what was wrong with her?"

"Mom didn't go to the doctor, because the clouds looked so bad that day. Your mother and I have been grateful that Susie hasn't gotten any worse these past few days."

Mom, Susie, and Matthew were safe at home all the time? That's the way I wanted it, but I certainly would have liked knowing it!

"How about a cup of coffee, Tony?" Mrs. Hart offered.

Dad unsnapped the chinstrap of his insulated hat and lifted one furry earflap to hear better. "Thanks, Vi, but we're heading right back. There's a layer of clouds up there that looks like it could develop into something. Has everything been okay here for you?"

"We've had plenty of food and plenty of help. Your girls are good helpers, Tony," said Mrs. Hart.

"Thanks again for taking care of them, Vi," Dad said. "We sure missed them at home. You have no idea how grateful Leona and I were to hear the announcement on the radio that they were here."

"They were worried about whether *you* and *Leona* made it home okay," she said.

Yeah, Dad! We *were worried about* you!

"Well, thank goodness Leona stayed home. I stopped at school that afternoon on the way home from Aberdeen, hoping to take them with me, but school had already let out. It took me a long time to get home. I couldn't see out the windshield, so the windows were down, with snow blowing in. I'm glad that I had chains with me to put on the tires."

"When *did* you hear the radio announcement about your girls being here?" Mrs. Hart asked.

"We heard it on the ten o'clock news the night of the snowstorm. Leona and I were worried, not knowing for a few hours. I debated going out to find them, but we decided to trust that they were okay. And thankfully, they were. We're grateful that you called the message in to the radio station."

"Are you thinking about getting a phone after this?" Mr. Hart asked.

Yeah! I could have had such a good time if we had a phone! I thought.

"No." He shook his head. "We get along fine without one. This just happens to be an unusual winter."

No, Dad! You *get along fine without one.*

"It's a harsh one," Mr. Hart agreed.

"These extra kids must have been a lot of work for you," Dad said, changing the subject.

"The girls pitched in and helped wherever they could," Mrs. Hart replied. "Like I said, they're good girls."

Carol, Kim, and I smiled when we heard those nice words from Mrs. Hart.

"Well, I'd better stop jawing and get back on the road. You girls all bundled up as warm as possible?"

We nodded. We had on our coats, mittens, dresses tucked into pants, pants tucked into overshoes, and scarves tied over our heads and around our necks. I was starting to feel a little warm in the porch.

"We'll head home, then," Dad said. "Much obliged, Joie, Vi!" He reached into his front overall pocket and handed Mr. Hart a folded piece of paper that looked like a check.

"Tony, this isn't necessary," Mr. Hart said.

"We're much obliged to you," Dad repeated, shaking his head when Mr. Hart tried to return the check. "Ready, girls?"

"Goodbye, girls," Mrs. Hart called as we left the house.

"'Bye," we answered.

"Thank you for everything!" Carol said.

"Thank you for everything!" Kim and I repeated.

As we walked to the tractor, David, Devon, and Dick came out of the barn to wave goodbye.

David yelled to me, "Hey, Rachel, we still have to get even with Devon and Dick!"

"Yes, we do! We have to think of something to really get back at them!" I waved and then said, "Bye!"

Dad looked at me with a question mark on his face. There was a gleam in his eye, too, for he sensed mischief. Then he climbed onto the tractor seat. Carol and Kim positioned themselves on the sides of the tractor seat, each with one foot on the axle and one on the hitching bar. I stood in the middle of the hitching bar behind the seat. All three of us had to find a grip on the seat, where there was little room because of Dad's big parka.

We'd better not hit any big bumps. A big one could send all three of us flying.

Dad started the tractor. "Are you set? Got a good hold?" he asked us. We nodded, and he shifted the tractor into gear and released the clutch slowly. We left the Hart farm and turned onto the highway.

Because of my position, I couldn't see what was ahead, so I looked to the rear. Snowbanks rose on both sides of us as solid white walls. They formed a long, narrow white canyon. It wasn't often on the flat prairie landscape that one had to look up to see the horizon, but I had to.

The tractor seemed to make good progress. At one point I saw a large indentation in the side of the snow wall. We moved away from it, and I realized it was one of the hollowed spaces that Mr. Hart had mentioned. Another mile up the road, Dad pulled the tractor into one of those spaces, and we waited for a few minutes. A pickup truck with a bandanna attached to the top of its aerial passed on and continued in the opposite direction.

"What's the handkerchief for?" I called.

"To help cars see one another at intersections," Dad answered. "When you see that bandanna moving above the snowbanks, you know a car is coming."

That made good sense to me.

The tractor had little difficulty traveling the highway. The heat directed at us from the comforter felt good and kept us from freezing. At one stop, I convinced Carol to trade places with me because there wasn't as much warmth getting behind the seat as at the sides. Kim took a turn on the hitching bar, too.

We were making slow but steady progress until we encountered the deep snow on the section road between the highway and the county road. Section roads were rarely maintained, except by the farmers who needed to use them, and this one was only used for farm field access by neighbors who owned land along it. The chains on the big tires were necessary to get us through this road. We had the advantage of the tracks Dad had forged on the way out, but we did encounter deep drifts of snow, and fear seized me every time the large wheels spun, the tractor hesitated, and the engine groaned, threatening to give up trying to conquer the drift.

Will we make it home? Or would we be a new headline:

Father and three daughters found frozen to tractor three miles from home?

When we finally arrived at our section road, travel was easier. Over the years, Dad had built our mile-long road up high, so when it snowed, the wind swept the snow off the road, down into the ditches, and up into drifts along the fencerow. The one place where this changed was the bend around the creek, at about the half-mile mark. Deep drifts often formed there when the wind blew from the north, as it did today.

"There it is, girls! Home!" Dad pointed to our farm on the rise a mile ahead.

"Yeah!" we said. We were too cold to yell and cheer.

Nevertheless, I stretched my neck to see over the comforter, and despite the cold wind and the anticipation of hard physical work again, an excitement went through me when I saw our farm on the rise. I was anxious to see Mom and Matthew and Susie.

We still had that bend in the road with its drifts to get through. I watched nervously as it came into view.

Chapter 14

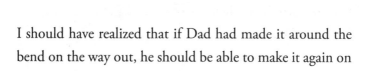

I should have realized that if Dad had made it around the bend on the way out, he should be able to make it again on the way back.

Snow had drifted across the road, filling in the deep tracks, but the tractor made it through the drifts.

After we crossed the iron bridge just past the bend, I saw high mounds of snow piled around the edge of the barnyard and in the cattle yard next to it, just as there were at the Harts'. In the farmyard, where the corncrib, the granary, the chicken house — without any chickens — the old garage, the Quonset grain bins, and another Quonset garage formed a semicircle to the north of the house, there were many more piles of snow. The center of the yard had been cleared for turnaround space, and snow had been removed from the fronts of the buildings so farm machines could have access to them. Dad must have put in many hours on the tractor with the hydraulic farmhand during the past few days to remove that much snow around the yard. And to think that he and Mom had done it without our help!

I must say I wasn't sorry to have missed all that work. One of my favorite things about staying with the Harts was that there had been plenty of other people to do the snow shoveling there.

I was glad we were only a quarter of a mile from home. The cold was starting to penetrate, and my hands and feet felt numb, so I wiggled them in my mittens and overshoes to stimulate circulation.

I tried to imagine the scenario inside the house while Mom and Susie waited for us. Mom would have guessed the time that she thought we would be coming home. She would have been looking out the kitchen window while working at the sink and counter, making something good for us to eat, the percolator bubbling with steaming coffee. Susie would have gone to the living-room window and watched the mile corner of our road for the very first sign of us. As she waited, she'd take time out now and then to talk excitedly to Matthew, who was probably either in his playpen or walking around holding on to the chairs and couches.

"It won't be long, Matthew Lee!" she'd say. "Daddy will be home. Rachel will be home. Kim will be home. And Carol will be home. All your big sisters — that includes me, you know — will be home."

Then she would probably walk to the kitchen to check on what Mom was doing and pester her about how much longer it would be before we would arrive.

And when she finally sighted us, she'd exclaim, "Mom! Mom! Here they come!" She'd squint her eyes against the brightness of the snow on this sunny day and follow our progress all the way.

I knew they were both watching us at this very minute as we made our way up the gentle hill on that last stretch of the road toward home.

When we turned into our lane, I stretched my neck to see over the comforter. I saw Mom, holding Matthew, and Susie at her side — all of them bundled up — waiting outside to greet us. Blackie, who had been trotting around them with his tail wagging, took running leaps in the deep snow toward us. How happy he, too, was to see us! Dad waved his thick-gloved hand at his welcoming wife and children. Susie waved and jumped up and down while Mom coaxed Matthew to wave.

Dad stopped the tractor by the garage driveway. "Here they are, Kid!" he said. Carol, Kim, and I climbed down from the tractor. My muscles were stiff from standing in the same position for so long.

Mom had a firm hold on Susie's hand so she wouldn't run to the tractor while the motor was running. "Hi, Rachel, Carol, Kim!" Susie called.

"Hi, Susie!" we hollered back.

When Dad shut the tractor off, Mom let go of Susie's hand and Susie rushed to us. Matthew was waving his baby hand up and down. He smiled and pointed. "Da Da!" His daddy, the tallest and most prominent among us with that big parka, was stiffly descending from the tractor.

Susie put her arms around me and hugged me tight.

"Missed me, huh?" I asked.

"Yup!" Then she hugged Carol and Kim.

The three of us took turns hugging Mom and Matthew at the same time.

A wave of heat rushed through me at the realization that this moment was a stark contrast to the other possibility I had envisioned for them — stranded on the road.

"It's good to have you home, girls," Mom said as she blinked back the tears welling in her eyes.

"It's good to be home!" we said, even me. And part of me meant it.

"That only took five hours both ways," Dad said. "It could have been worse. The chains made the difference. There's still only one lane on the highway. The banks along Highway 45 are as high as your head. This snow is going to be here for a long time."

"All of you must be chilled to the bone! Let's go in and get you warmed up." Mom led us into the breezeway, where we took off our coats and overshoes before stepping up into the warm kitchen.

The aroma of hot cinnamon rolls just out of the oven greeted us.

"Boy, those cinnamon rolls smell good, Mom," I said. Mom smiled at me. She knew they were a favorite of ours, and especially of mine. A large pot of vegetable soup — surely with lots of our canned garden tomatoes, beans, carrots, and potatoes, and chunks of our own corn-fed beef in it — simmered on the stove. Steam was spouting from the coffeepot, adding to the wonderful mixture of smells in the air.

We sat around the table, eating and exchanging storm stories. The radio was set at low volume, a background to our conversation.

When the weather report came on, Dad said, "Quiet everyone!" Since Kim was nearest to the radio, Dad ordered, "Kim, turn that up, please."

I did not like what I heard. None of us did. More snow and wind were in the forecast.

I kept my groans to myself.

Chapter 15

We woke up the next morning to high winds and blowing snow that played hide-and-seek with the landscape beyond our windows.

Six inches of new snow had fallen during the night. I'm certain that I heard the first *whoosh* of the wind in the early morning hours — probably after the snow stopped falling.

The wind could blow all around our house, but it couldn't so much as rattle the windows. Our house was built just two years earlier, tight and sturdy and faced with four-inch-thick Minnesota limestone.

I felt safe and warm inside. The hot-water baseboard registers along the walls kept us warm even in the coldest weather. But outside this morning there was a very different situation. The near-zero temperature and fierce winds made the weather bitter cold and dangerous.

The sky had a frigid blue tint, and the wind was whipping the fine white crystals into a fury around the buildings and between the snow mounds. Any snow that had been blown into drifts was being dispersed by the mighty wind and sent searching for a new place to rest.

The haymow and peak of the barn's roof remained visible against the clear sky, but the lower part of the barn appeared and disappeared in the swirling snow. The weatherman had called it a ground blizzard.

I dreaded the idea of getting out for chores in this horrible weather, but for some reason, to my delight, Dad decided that I didn't have to — only Kim and Carol had to help him this morning.

"Make sure your faces are covered," Mom warned. "That wind and cold snow will beat your skin raw."

Susie and I watched from the corner kitchen windows as the three bundled forms headed down the hill toward the barnyard to feed hay and corn to the cattle and check the water supply, since all two hundred head of cattle were in the two barnyards.

I felt some pangs of guilt while watching from the cozy house. After seeing how the wind buffeted Dad, Carol, and Kim, I wondered if perhaps Dad thought I couldn't hold my weight against it. I had a slight build — an advantage at times, but it also limited my strength.

The severity of what the three of them faced was daunting. I imagined them trying to pitch the hay against the force of the wind without being blown off the stacks themselves. That would require strength and careful timing between gusts. Keeping the flying alfalfa leaves out of their eyes would be hard, too. Then, to get the hay to fall into the proper place inside the corral would also be tricky.

At one point the gusts stopped briefly and I saw cattle huddled together in the metal windbreak shed. At the barn, steam from the cattle's breath and the heat of their bodies rolled out of the one open door.

Carol and Kim were pitching hay in the south cattle yard, but I saw no sign of Dad. He wasn't at the feed wagon, and no cattle lined the feed bunks. I had a feeling that he decided to skip that feeding because the wind would blow the fine grain out of the scoop shovel and also out of the shallow bunk.

Susie got tired of watching and left to entertain Matthew in the living room.

For a brief moment, there was a break in the high winds, and just before they resumed, I caught a glimpse of Dad swinging the ax to chop holes in the ice on the cattle's water tank. The cattle could eat snow for water in an emergency, but a frozen, clogged line to the tank could also lead to water problems in our house.

With the artesian well, the water flowed naturally — that meant uphill to the house. It was a slow trickle that fell into the supply tank in the house on most days. In winter it was often less than a trickle. And if the line froze, the house would not *have* water.

The house was quiet, so I opened the kitchen door above the stairway to the basement and listened for the water flowing into the tank in the utility room. It had slowed to a drip. *Not good!* I didn't relish the idea of using the old outhouse. I had gotten accustomed to modern plumbing.

I closed the door and returned to my post at the window, but not for long. I heard Mom being sick in the bathroom. Susie and I ran from different directions to help.

Mom was never sick. The new sound startled Matthew, and he began crying in the living room.

"Mom, what's wrong?" I asked at the bathroom door when I saw her on her knees in front of the stool.

"I'm okay," she said.

"But you're sick," Susie said.

"I'm okay," she said again.

There was something familiar about this scene, and I began to suspect that I knew why Mom was ill.

Not again! I thought.

Chapter 16

When Dad, Carol, and Kim returned to the house after feeding the cattle, their face scarves and Dad's parka flap were frosty white from their frozen breath. The cold had so penetrated their bodies that it was difficult for them to remove their wraps.

Susie had watched them from the kitchen window as they entered the breezeway, and she was right there to greet the shivering trio when they came up the steps to the kitchen. They barely got through the door when she announced, "Mom got sick!"

"Susie!" I reprimanded.

"Well, she did!" She didn't realize the sensitivity of the situation.

"Kid?" Dad questioned.

"It isn't anything," she said. I could tell that he knew, and a worried look crossed his face.

"It isn't anything. I'm okay," she reassured him.

Carol, Kim, and I exchanged knowing glances. We knew better than to react the way we had when we discovered Mom was pregnant with Matthew. We had been appalled. Mom had been hurt by our reaction, and Dad was mad. Yet I wondered if Carol and Kim were thinking similar thoughts to mine. *Another baby! We already have more kids in our family than anyone else!*

Whatever our thoughts, we girls kept them to ourselves and waited expectantly for the announcement, the explanation of Mom's sickness.

Finally Carol asked, "Are you going to tell Susie?"

"Tell me what?"

"That *you* are going to have another little brother or sister," Mom answered. "Your dad and I thought it would be nice for Matthew to have a little brother or sister nearer his age to grow up with."

"Oh!" Susie thought for a few seconds and then said, "I *am* a lot older than he is."

I remembered how quickly Matthew was born, and with little warning. *What if there's a blizzard when it's time?*

"When?" I asked.

"Not until April," Mom answered.

"That's a relief. This is a terrible winter to have a baby," I said. I noticed that the worried look was still on Dad's face.

The rest of the day was rather somber for our family. In midafternoon Susie and I sat together, our backs absorbing the heat from the baseboard registers. She read her *Jack and Jill* magazine and I read my *Teen* magazine.

I was amused when I overheard Susie tell Matthew that he was going to have a little brother or sister. "In April, Matthew Lee, you are going to have a baby brother or sister. Winter will be over then. The baby is growing in your mommy's tummy. She and Daddy will go to the hospital and then come home with a baby boy or baby girl."

Matthew appeared to listen intently. He smiled his happy toddler smile. When he heard the word *Daddy*, he pointed at Dad in his lounge chair reading his *Newsweek* and said, "Da Da!"

"Yes, that's Daddy," Susie said.

When Matthew heard *Mom* or *Mommy*, he said, "Mah?" and looked around. When he heard her working in the kitchen, he smiled and pointed to that arched door and said, "Mah!"

"That's right! Mommy! Now, Matthew Lee, which would you rather have — a brother or a sister?"

He looked at her and smiled.

"*I* would rather have a brother. I already have *three* sisters."

"And what's wrong with sisters?" I asked.

"Nothing. But I have three and only one brother."

Just then Mom ran to the bathroom and was sick again. Dad lowered his magazine. The worried look was back on his face.

To make matters worse, winter was relentless for the next two weeks. Snow and wind and more snow and wind. We were off school the whole time. I hated it and grew short-tempered. I snapped at everyone until Dad said, "I think you need to do a bigger share of the chores to sweeten you up."

"Sweeten her up? Ha!" Kim mocked.

I resisted a nasty comeback. Dad's threat of more chores in weather like this might not sweeten me up, but I would think twice before I barked at anyone.

One morning, a cold blue sky and calm winds were welcome weather despite the fact that I was assigned with Kim to help pitch hay. Dad chopped ice off the water tank and fed hay from the haymow. Carol fed the ground corn. The cattle eagerly ran to vie for spaces along the feed banks. They came to eat hay, too, but the dried alfalfa apparently wasn't as enticing as ground corn.

I'd like ground corn better, too, if I were a cow. The color is better. The powdery corn has to be sweeter and easier to eat than dried stems and leaves.

After feeding the cattle, Dad spent the rest of the morning removing snow from around our yard with the farmhand scoop and dumping it down by the creek.

When asked why this was necessary, he explained, "When all the snow melts next spring, I'd rather have it run into the creek than downhill into the cattle yards. I don't want my cattle knee deep in . . . soupy manure."

While he was removing the snow, two of the gates in the cattle yard needed to be open so he could get down to the creek. Carol was helping Mom in the house, so Kim and I each got the job of guarding a gate so the cattle wouldn't escape. The gates were positioned close enough so we could talk to each other.

"Is this really necessary?" Kim complained.

"It is if you don't want to wade through you know

what kind of mud next spring to get to the haystack and feed wagon."

"It's cold, and this is a boring job."

It *was* cold. To keep warm, I started moving around, swinging my arms, stamping my toes, and clapping my mittens together. Then I decided to do some cheerleading routines that I'd seen Carol and the other high school and junior high cheerleaders perform. Routines were more fun than just moving.

As for boring, I preferred it that way. Dealing with cattle was the kind of work that could turn much too exciting in a matter of seconds. None of us needed that kind of excitement right now.

From time to time, the cattle followed the tractor toward the gates, because often Dad carried feed or mineral blocks in the farmhand and even used it as a lure to bring them home from the pasture. I waved a stick and hollered at them when they tried to follow now.

The sunlight reflected from the white snow made a very bright day. My eyes did a lot of squinting, and my face got a snowburn. My cheeks were red-hot.

As we were closing the gates at lunchtime, we heard an

engine overhead. Someone was flying a small airplane. The airplane circled over our farm a couple of times, then flew lower. When it banked to the side, we recognized the pilot.

"Herbie!" Kim and I exclaimed.

Herbie Conlon was our farm neighbor two miles north, "as the crow flies," as Dad would say.

"He has skis on instead of wheels!"

"Easier to land on snow with skis," Kim said, her tone indicating that that should be obvious.

Herbie turned and buzzed us. He was motioning with his hands.

"I think he plans to land," I said.

He circled east and turned back, descending and then landing in the alfalfa field southeast of the house.

Dad watched the landing, still sitting on the tractor. Mom, Carol, and Susie were taking this all in behind the big picture window. Dad dismounted from the tractor and walked to meet Herbie in the field as he climbed out of his Piper Cub. Kim and I trudged behind, hoping to learn what this visit was about.

"Herbie, this is a surprise." Dad took off his right glove to shake hands.

"Girls." Herbie acknowledged Kim and me with a nod of the head. Then he asked Dad, "How are you, Leona, and the rest of the family?"

"We're doing fine. I suspect this isn't a social call, though," Dad said with a little chuckle. "Do you have time for a cup of coffee?"

"I'd better pass, Tony, thanks. I'll get right to the point."

Dad nodded that he understood. Kim and I were all ears.

"I'm on the school board, you know, and we had a meeting over the phones, so to speak, last night. The kids have missed a lot of school and likely will miss more in days and weeks to come."

"It's been severe, and there's a lot of winter left," Dad agreed.

"As you know, the majority of our schoolchildren live on farms, and the board would like those children to move into town so we can continue school."

Kim nudged me with her elbow. Our eyes met, wide with surprise.

"We've notified most of the parents by phone, but I flew out today to check for a landing spot so I could tell you, too. You also know that our school band has been invited to the Midwest Band Clinic in Chicago next December. We would like to see that still happen, and the band needs a lot of rehearsal before they are ready to perform in Chicago. If the kids are in town, they can rehearse. You have three children in the school's forty-piece band, and each is important."

"Well"— Dad hesitated —"I'm not sure. Our kids are a big help to us. I'll have to talk this over with Leona. If we let them go, I don't know when we could get them safely to town."

"That's why I'm here. I'll be happy to come back tomorrow and fly them in. The good weather is supposed to hold another day."

"Let me go check quick with Leona and see how she feels. If they go, we don't have any relatives in town for them to stay with. Is there a room at the hotel? We'd be willing to rent a room there."

"I'm sure, but I'll check that out for you, Tony, before I come back."

"I'll be back shortly," Dad said.

Staying in town? There's a possibility of staying in town! Oh, Mom, please let us go! I was overjoyed at the thought of being in town.

I turned to Kim. "What do you think?" I asked softly.

"Fifty-fifty chance," she said.

"Yeah," I agreed.

"It's a lot of work, isn't it?" Herbie said to us. "Taking care of the livestock with all this snow and cold."

"Yes, it is!" I said. "Do Laura and Karla help outside?" Laura was in Kim's class, and Karla was in fifth-grade.

"Yes, they help, but we don't have many cattle this winter, so it's not as much work as you have."

We heard the house door close and saw Dad making his way toward the airplane. I tried to tell by his expression what the decision was.

"Well, we're going to try to get along without our girls," Dad said.

I controlled my urge to jump up and down for joy, but every inch of me shivered with excitement. *I hope Mom and Dad never find out what a rotten daughter I am.*

"I know it will be hard, Tony, without a telephone to keep in touch with them, but there will be a lot of good people to help look out for your girls."

"Leona and I know that. Otherwise we wouldn't let them go."

"There is one thing, Tony," Herbie said. "I have room

for only three. Many folks are keeping their younger children home — those younger than third-grade."

"Oh, my! Susie's not going to like that," Dad said, shaking his head.

Poor, poor Susie! I was sad for her. *Poor Dad! He has to break the news to her.*

Chapter 17

I got ready for my stay in town.

How I was looking forward to being back with Winnie and Melissa and Darren! Being in the middle of things and knowing what was going on would be great. Afterschool get-togethers and whole weekends in town had always seemed like such fun. I'd finally get to go tobogganing at Cresbard Lake. It wouldn't matter if I had a phone or not, but maybe there would be one in the hotel. And no chores to do! I liked the thought of doing whatever I wanted to, whenever I wanted to — except when school was in session. Then Mrs. Kelly ruled.

My joy was dampened a bit by a twinge of guilt when I thought of Dad and Mom dealing with all the chores by themselves in this brutal winter — and Mom being pregnant and sometimes sick. And I was sad for Susie, who was crushed that she would be left behind.

She sobbed when she heard the news, tears streaming down her cheeks. "Mama, why can't *I* go to town to school?"

Mom tried to explain. "They don't have enough room on the airplane, sweetie."

"Why don't they get a *bigger* airplane?" she asked, still sobbing.

"It's not that simple, honey. Airplanes are very expensive, and Herbie is lucky to have a small one of his own. Besides, you heard your daddy. He said that Herbie told him a lot of families were keeping their younger children home."

"It's not fair. I love school."

"I know you do, Susie, but we'll do schoolwork here at home."

"It's not the same. I like doing schoolwork with kids." Her nose was starting to run with her tears.

Mom got out her hankie and dabbed at Susie's tears. "Here, sweetie, blow your nose."

After Susie blew her nose, Mom hugged her and said, "Honey, I'm so happy that you will be home to help me. I especially need your help with Matthew. You are such a good sister to him, and he loves you. Do you know how much he would miss you if you were gone for a long time?"

"Yes," Susie finally said, and her sobbing lessened. She came to me and hugged me. "I'm going to miss you, Rachel."

I hugged her back. "I'm going to miss you, too, Susie."

Susie stopped crying, but the sparkle was missing from her brown eyes.

Matthew toddled over to Mom and Susie just then.

"Come here, Matthew!" Susie said, holding her hands out for him. He went to her and she took his hands. "I'm going to be your only big sister at home for a while. What do you think of that?"

He gave her a huge grin and asked a question in baby talk.

"That's right, Matthew!" Susie answered, interpreting his baby talk as she pleased. "It'll be just you and me and Mom and Dad."

I knew Susie's heart was breaking, and I was sorry, but I was elated by the idea of my first airplane ride *and* staying in town morning, noon, and night. The next day, I was up early, checking and rechecking the clothes that I would take, making sure I had my toothbrush and hairbrush and bobby pins. I was so excited that it was hard to eat the hearty breakfast of eggs, sausage patties, and pancakes that Mom had made.

The clothes for all three of us were packed in the only suitcase Mom had. There had been little water in the supply tank, so yesterday only one small load of wash — all of our underpants, bras for Kim and Carol, T-shirts for me — was done in our wringer washing machine. The rest we washed by hand, which uses less water, and hung on a line to dry in the basement. Getting to the outdoor clothesline was too difficult in this weather. Besides, the wind would have wrapped the clothes around the line, and they would have frozen there.

Mom said that this hand washing was a practice run because that's how we would have to do it in the hotel. She included laundry detergent powder for us in the suitcase.

Midmorning, we heard the airplane motor and saw its shadow circle on the snow. We heard the engine shut down, and from the big picture window we watched the airplane descend and land in the same field where Herbie had landed the day before.

I was filled with anticipation and a little fear at the prospect of the plane ride ahead.

When I turned away from the window to leave, Susie

hugged me hard, reluctant to let go. I realized then that I *would* really miss her.

"I wish I could go," she said softly, a quiver in her voice.

"I wish you could, too." We held together until Mom — looking pale, I noticed — came to give me a hug. Mom gave me a lingering embrace and a kiss on the cheek. The faint scent of baby powder on her triggered something in me.

I wanted to whisper, *I'll miss you, Mom,* but I knew that my voice would crack and I would start to cry. I let her go so she could hug and kiss Kim and Carol. As we left the house, tears were in her eyes. She held Matthew in one arm, and the other was around Susie.

Dad, carrying the suitcase, soberly walked us to the airplane. Carol, Kim, and I each clasped brown paper sacks filled with miscellaneous personal stuff. Earlier Dad had given us each a little spending money and had given Carol a check to pay for our hotel room and board.

I looked back at the house and waved, knowing Mom and Susie would be watching from the big window. That forlorn look on Susie's face and her halfhearted wave saddened me.

Mom held Matthew and pointed to us. *Please let her sickness be over.*

When we neared the plane, Herbie jumped out and held the door open. He indicated that the suitcase was to go behind the back seat, so Dad, ducking to avoid the metal bars that braced the wing, stowed it there. As he started to back away, I stepped on my tiptoes and gave Dad a quick kiss on his cheek.

"Bye, Dad!" I said.

"Yeah, bye," he said softly. Then Kim and I climbed into the back seat and Carol sat in the seat beside the pilot's.

"There's a room at the hotel for the girls, then, Herbie?" he asked.

"Yes. They said they'd have their room ready for them today."

"Much obliged," Dad said, and then shook Herbie's hand.

"Do you and Leona need anything, Tony? Some of the farmers around needed extra supplies," Herbie said.

"No. We canned a lot from our garden last summer, and our freezer is full of beef. Just hope the electricity doesn't go out. We have plenty of hay for the cattle, too. We're going to miss our girls. They are a big help around here," he added.

"I know they are. Wish you had a phone, Tony, in case you need something out here."

"Ah, well . . ." Dad said.

Kim and I rolled our eyes at each other. I thought about Mom, who was still standing in the window with Matthew and Susie. *I wish we had a phone for Mom's sake.*

Before jumping into the pilot's seat, Herbie gave the propeller a downward push and started it spinning. Dad stepped away from the plane as Herbie closed his door.

"Goodbye, girls!" he called, his words muffled by the propellor noise. He waved his big gloved hand.

"Bye, Dad!" we shouted back. If he couldn't hear us over the engine, he could read our lips.

Herbie manipulated the controls, and the engine revved and the propellers spun faster. The whole airplane shook with vibrations and started moving forward.

Kim and I gripped the seatbacks in front of us. Carol calmly looked out the front and side windows.

The engine revved more; then we moved forward faster and faster as the propellers became a whirring, circular blur. Just as it seemed the plane would shake apart, the nose eased up, and soon the machine was free of the ground.

I felt a tickle in my stomach as the plane soared upward. The violent vibrating stopped, and the roar of the engine enveloped us. Herbie banked and turned and circled above the farm, tipping a wing toward the house, giving us one last glimpse of Dad and Mom, who had stepped outside with Matthew and Susie, all of them waving at us.

Blackie was there, too, barking up at the airplane.

Then the plane leveled and headed toward town. Our house, the small backs of the cattle in the yard, the white farm buildings surrounded by piles of snow, and the shiny peaked roofs of the metal granaries slipped away beneath us. Mom and Dad became tiny specks. The buildings became miniature structures, resembling the houses on a Monopoly board. Down by the creek, the old junk pile looked like a heap of black ashes poking through the snow.

We climbed higher, then leveled again. In the morning sun, the snaking curve of the winding creek was outlined by the shadow of the high east banks. Out the side window I saw a grove of trees and recognized the farm of our neighbor Will Hall. His farm buildings were closer together than ours were. The tops of the evergreen trees, which surrounded his house and lined the lane to the county road, flared out at the bottoms like circle skirts. Then we flew over Herbie's farm. His buildings were closer together, too, and his house was near a well-maintained section road.

Each farm had a blackened spot around the barns where the cattle had tromped in the snow.

"Laura and Karla are staying in town with their grandmother," Herbie shouted over the engine. "I flew them in yesterday."

We nodded to let him know that we heard him.

The winding creek meandered from our place through the farmlands toward town. I was amazed at how like a snake it was. *No wonder it's called Snake Creek.* I nudged Kim and pointed to the toylike snowplow creeping on the county road below. My eyes squinted against the bright reflection of the snow everywhere beneath us. Barely poking through the snow, the tops of the fence posts that separated farm fields looked like faint dotted lines making large squares on white paper.

This is so much more fun than riding to town in a car! I can see so far.

"I see the Mackeys' place!" I shouted. Kim leaned toward my window to see.

"It looks like they've pulled the bus out of the snowbank!" She pointed to the corner where it had been stuck.

"There's the Harts' farm and the Kahns' farm!" They looked like patches of gray and red on a vast white landscape. It took me a while to recognize them, because I was seeing them from an unfamiliar place.

Everything looks so much smaller from up here.

Kim wasn't listening to me anymore. She and Carol were engrossed, too, by what they were seeing out their windows.

We approached the familiar skyline of Cresbard — a row of tall wooden grain elevators on the south side of town. Herbie circled the town and began the descent. From the air, we could see that the town was laid out in a grid behind that front line of elevators. Main Street, running north and south, was paralleled by one street to the west and two to the east and crossed by six streets. Each square in the grid was outlined with buildings.

The school, the largest building in town aside from the elevators, was easy to spot on the northeast edge of town. There were even a few kids on the playground. Because their farms were close to school, I spotted Melissa's and Winnie's farms. At the dead end of Main Street, where every day our bus turned toward the school, there was a giant snowman in the front yard of Darren Baxter's house.

From the airplane, the water tower, second tallest structure to the elevators, did not look as imposing as it did from the ground looking up at it. Just a half block to the north was the hotel.

My town home! I thought. I knew it wouldn't be fancy. The two-story frame building looked as old as the town — fifty years. The merchants were already planning the town's fifty-year celebration to be held in the summer.

Herbie was completing the wide circle around town. He moved some controls, the engine quieted, and we slowed. The nose pitched slightly toward the ground, and the plane descended, heading toward the row of grain elevators. A tickling rush danced in my stomach, reminding me of the thrill when a car drove fast down a short steep hill. The plane slowed some more. I gasped when the electric wires and poles along Highway 20 passed under us.

Too close for comfort!

"Prepare yourselves for a bump!" Herbie warned. The ground drew closer and closer and closer. I held on tight. Bump! We had made contact. The vibrating began, then eased as Herbie piloted the skiing plane down his landing strip on the alfalfa field near town. The plane slowed, then came to a stop.

"Here we are, girls! How'd you like the ride?" Herbie asked before opening his door.

"I liked it!" I said.

"It was great!" Kim said.

"Yes, it was!" Carol said.

"Good!" he replied. "I'll be flying back to my farm, so it looks like you'll have to walk from here." He opened his door and got out and held it for Kim and me. Kim struggled with the big suitcase behind us while I jumped down, holding the hand that Herbie offered to help.

"I'll get that," Herbie said, helping Kim down first and then retrieving the suitcase.

"Thank you! It's heavy!" Kim said.

Carol jumped down from her door and came around to our side of the plane.

"Thank you very much, Herbie!" she said.

"Yes, thank you!" said Kim.

"Thank you from me, too!" I added.

"You're all welcome, girls. If you need anything, please let me know."

Carol lifted the suitcase, and we headed to the hotel.

Here we are in town! This should be so much fun!

Chapter 18

We followed the shoveled lane from the airstrip, past the livestock sale barn that sat alone at the edge of town, past the implement dealer, to the beginning of the narrow shoveled path on the sidewalk.

The banks on either side were above my waist, and a lot of snow had fallen from them back into the sidewalk path. That made navigating the narrow channel difficult. Walking single file, Kim and Carol took turns carrying the suitcase. I carried the three paper sacks — one under each arm and one in my hand, last in line as always, a fate I was getting tired of.

Heaps of snow were piled on both sides of the wide street and some in the middle. A few cars were parked diagonally between the heaps.

We passed the lumber company and the gas station, which was on the opposite side of the street. Then we crossed to the next block, where only one customer sat at the U-shaped counter of John's Diner.

I can come down here and get nickel ice cream cones with some of the spending money Dad gave us. I won't have to sneak into the freezer downstairs and eat ice cream on the sly. Then I smiled. *I wonder if Mom will miss finding the half-empty ice cream cartons.*

Mr. Harris, owner of Mel's Market next door to John's Diner, was trying to remove packed snow from the sidewalk in front of his grocery store. He stopped when we passed.

"How was the plane ride, girls? Herbie said he was flying you in today."

"It was good," Carol said. She set the suitcase down.

"It was our first plane ride," Kim added.

"The plane shook a lot at first," I said.

"And how are your folks?" he asked.

"They're fine," Carol answered.

I was glad that Susie wasn't there to blurt out that Mom was going to have another baby. None of us would tell it, because we were embarrassed about it.

"So you're bunking at the hotel?" Mr. Harris asked.

"We don't have any relatives in town, and the hotel has a room we can rent, so Dad thought that was where we should stay," Carol explained.

"I hope it doesn't get too cold. They don't have heat upstairs," Mr. Harris said.

I grimaced. "We know. Mom told us."

"Well, girls, if you need anything or want anything, you can charge it here and your dad can pay later."

"Thank you," Carol said. Kim and I smiled our thanks.

"My turn," Kim said, picking up the suitcase with both hands. It hit against her leg as she walked. "Hey, Rachel! You should be able to take a turn with the suitcase," she added.

"Nope! Don't want to."

We passed the barbershop and the Bank of Cresbard; then we crossed the main intersection that divided the town. The lace curtains that went halfway up the windows were closed in the Cresbard Café. Only one car was parked in front.

The next store was the pool hall. The sign painted on the window said RECREATION PARLOR, and I wondered why it said that when everyone called it the pool hall. Dad played cards in there with other men sometimes. It smelled like beer, smoke, and oiled wood floor. There were no cars in front of the hardware store or mercantile store and no sign of any customers.

Next in line was the water tower with CRESBARD printed on it. It looked so high from the ground.

At the end of that block, the town's caboose library, painted white, stood guard on the abandoned rails. The sign on the door said it was open only on Saturday afternoons. All I had to do now was walk across the street to check out books and comic books. Mrs. Stein, the volunteer librarian, was always so sweet to me.

My focus went from the caboose to the two-story white frame building sitting on the corner of the next block. I stopped and gazed at it. On some of the boards, gray wood peeked out behind patches of peeling white paint. HOTEL was painted in large, faded black letters across the façade above the storefront. CAFÉ was printed in yellow writing on the window. It didn't seem very homey.

Looking up at the second-story windows, where the rooms without heat were, I asked, "Which room do you think is ours?"

"Come on, Rachel!" Kim snapped at me.

"Aren't you curious?"

"We'll find out soon. Come on!"

She and Carol had crossed the street and were waiting by the door. I hesitated, then hurried to join them, the sacks rustling and about ready to drop from my arms. I thought it best not to test their authority here, now. Kim set the suitcase down by the door, and she opened it so Carol could carry the suitcase in. I held the outside door with my back, and Kim opened the inside door.

We scraped our feet on the rug by the door. Then I cased the joint, as Winnie would say, by checking out the details of the hotel café.

Three dark brown varnished wooden booths sat unoccupied along the front wall. The middle booth received sunshine from the only window along that wall. The rest of the room had little light. On the opposite side, swivel-top stools with red vinyl seats lined a counter. Burn spots from cigarettes randomly dotted the speckled gray linoleum that covered it.

I plopped the cumbersome paper sacks on the table of the nearest booth and sat on the edge of the bench. On the tabletop sat a napkin holder, salt- and peppershakers, and ketchup and mustard bottles in place against the wall. D.P. + J.O. was carved in the varnished dark wood seat.

"Carol, come here! Do you think this is Dan Peters plus Jenny Oswald?" I asked.

"I'll look later, Rachel. Here come the Stewarts." Carol had stepped up to the counter after we walked in, assuming her oldest-sister, take-charge responsibility. She could see down the hallway that led from the café to the living quarters.

A shadow crossed an inner doorway and was followed by the appearance of a short, dark-haired lady who was wiping her hands on her apron. Behind her was an elderly man with graying hair. He switched on the light, and that brightened the room.

"Hello, girls! I've been expecting you," the lady said in a pleasant voice. "Herbie called me yesterday to let me know your dad wanted a room for you. And we have one. So far, you are our only renters."

"Hello, Mrs. Stewart," Carol said.

"Call me Mabel. Everybody does."

"Mabel," Carol repeated, as though trying to get used to it. "I'm Carol, and this is Kim, and Rachel's in the booth."

"Welcome, girls. This is my husband, Frank."

"Howdy, girls!" Frank said with a friendly smile.

"Howdy!" I said back. Kim elbowed me for my boldness.

"Mrs. — Mabel," Carol started while reaching into her pocket for her billfold. "Dad gave me this check as a deposit for our room and meals."

"That's good of your dad. I appreciate it."

"He'll pay the rest when he can come to town," Carol added.

Mabel smiled. "This has been quite a winter!" She pulled down a lever on the ornate upright cash register, which was higher than she was. The drawer at the bottom popped out to the sound of a bell, and Mabel placed the check in one of the partitions and closed the drawer.

"How was the plane ride?" she asked. "Your first?"

"It was our first, and it was good," Carol answered.

Kim and I nodded in agreement.

"Come. I'll show you your room. You can take your overshoes off and set them here." She pointed to a rag rug by the door, and we took off our overshoes.

Then Mabel led us up a steep walled staircase at the side of the building. Carol followed, with Kim behind her, helping her hold one end of the suitcase. I followed them all. The staircase smelled of dust mixed with food grease. We walked down the hallway to the second door on the right. Mabel opened the door. I held my breath, thinking it would be dim and dingy like the café was, without lights.

But the light coming through the window, which over-looked Main Street, gave the room an unexpected clean and airy feeling. The floorboards were painted a tan color. The wallpaper was a light tan with columns of pink flowers and green leaves. Along one wall was a wooden wardrobe and chest of drawers side by side. In the middle of the room was a bed with a blue and white patchwork quilt. An oval rag rug was on each side. In warmer weather, the room would have been cheery.

"I put three quilts on, girls," said Mabel. "We don't have a stove up here, and it does get cold at night. There's a little heat that rises through this grate, though." She pointed to the square metal grill with curlicue holes in it that was in the floor by the wall. "You can do your homework at the booths downstairs. You really only have to sleep and dress in this room." She pointed to the open door across the hall, where there was a sink and toilet and three towels folded over a rack. "There's the washroom. I'm sorry we don't have hot water up here. You can use this pitcher and bowl when you wash up in the morning."

The pitcher and bowl were sitting on a small wooden table in our room. Blue towels and washcloths hung over wooden dowels on each side.

"You know, I think Frank and I can accommodate one more in the mornings in our bathroom, where there is hot water. Perhaps Rachel, since she is the youngest."

"Yeah, that's fine with me!" *Why wouldn't it be?*

Carol and Kim said nothing.

"Of course, for your Saturday night baths, you may each use our bathtub," Mabel added. "It's almost noon and time for dinner. Why don't you put your things away and then come down and order something to eat," she suggested.

We thanked her and hung our hanging things in the wardrobe and placed the rest of our things in the chest of drawers.

"Why do I always get the bottom drawer?" I complained.

"Because you're the youngest," Kim said.

"Hmpf!" I grunted. "Maybe I should have the top drawer because I'm the youngest." But I placed my undershirts, underpants, socks, pajamas, and two hankies in the designated drawer.

Soon we were on our way back down the narrow staircase. When we entered the café, no one was there except us. Mabel brought three glasses of water to the counter where we sat on the swivel stools. "Order anything you like, girls," she said.

Soon we were biting into hamburgers with pickles and ketchup, french fries dabbed in ketchup, and everything swallowed with milk.

This is like eating out. We're going to be eating out every day! Our family didn't go out to cafés to eat. Sometimes we girls would have a hamburger with friends at the Cresbard Café after ball games before going home. A few times, if we were in Aberdeen for a livestock sale, Dad would stop at an A&W Root Beer drive-in and we'd order hamburgers, french fries, and root beer. The carhop would bring our order to the car and place a tray with special clips on Dad's lowered window. Dad would pay, and we'd eat in the car until we were finished and then place our used napkins, plastic dishes, and root beer mugs back on the tray for the carhop to take away. We had hamburgers at home and beef roasts and T-bone steaks because we had cattle, but french fries and root beer were a real treat.

"Any dessert for you, girls?" Mabel asked when she came to clear our dishes.

"Do you have lemon meringue pie?" I asked.

"Not today," she answered.

"Then no dessert for me."

"Me neither," Kim said.

"Nor me," Carol said.

She frowned. "Don't any of you like desserts?"

"Rachel does. She likes them," Kim offered.

"Maybe tomorrow I'll make some lemon pie," Mabel said, smiling at me.

I grinned back. "Where are all the kids that are supposed to be in town?" I asked.

"The school has been open for the past two days so they have someplace to go," Mabel answered. "They use the gym, and the band kids practice in the band room. A noon meal is served up there, too."

I couldn't wait to see my friends.

"Let's go check it out!" I said.

After lunch, our walk to the school took us past three blocks of residences where Main Street dead-ended at the north end of town in front of Darren Baxter's house. The school was on the second block to the east and the only building on the whole block. Then the fields began.

When we turned onto the street toward the school, we heard the excited voices of kids playing outside. There were groups of younger kids running around a new pie circle that had been shuffled in the snow, playing fox and goose, and there was an impressive large snow fort and a small animal snow sculpture that looked like a polar bear.

The three of us didn't spot any of our friends on the playground, so we entered the school and heard basketballs bouncing in the gym downstairs, accompanied by energetic voices. We went down and watched the kids who were shooting hoops for fun.

"Hey, Rachel, how was the flight?" David called from the spot where he was attempting a long shot.

"Good one, David!" I clapped when he made it. "The flight was good, too!"

"See you later!" he said.

"Yeah," I replied.

Strains of "Rhapsody in Blue" came from the Quonset band room, an addition behind the sturdy two-story brick school and accessed from the gym through a long uphill hallway.

"The band's practicing!" Carol exclaimed.

Hurrying along the gymnasium wall, we dodged basketballs as they dropped through the hoop or bounced off the rim. Then we dashed up the hallway. *Oh, to play my coronet again. Carol and Kim have to feel the same. It's been over two weeks!* Our instruments, we called them horns for short, had been left in the band room in the emergency dismissal. Carol played the baritone horn and Kim the clarinet.

At home, we usually practiced our horns in the basement living room, which was really a playroom. Mr. Klitz, our band director, had high expectations of his students, and we practiced every night.

The thought of home returned, and for a brief minute I hoped that everything was okay with Mom, Dad, Susie, and Matthew. I also experienced a pang of guilt because I felt so happy to be here. As I nearly skipped up the hallway to the band room, the swell of music sent shivers through me.

When we opened the door, Mr. Klitz greeted us with a big smile, and the kids' eyes glanced at us over their music. Mr. Klitz tapped his baton on the music stand in front of him, and the band obeyed his signal to stop.

"Hello, Johnson girls!" he greeted us.

"Hi, Rachel! Hi, Kim! Hi, Carol!" various band members called out to us.

I heard Winnie's voice, and Melissa's, and even Darren's from the trombone section.

"Hi, everyone!" we greeted in return.

"I am so glad to see you!" Mr. Klitz said. "Your horns should be along the wall at the back. Join in when you're ready. We'll start back at section two," he said to the band. He raised his baton and moved it to a one-two-three-four count to give them the beat, and the band started playing.

We found our horn cases, removed our instruments, and warmed up by quietly blowing air through the mouthpieces.

While I was warming up, my line of vision ran directly to Darren, who, with no notes to play for several measures, held his trombone down at his side. I was flustered when I saw him smiling at me.

I returned a quick, nervous smile and then took my seat in the coronet section. Carol and Kim had taken their seats, too. We found the place on the music sheets and added our horns to the harmony.

Chapter 19

Band practice lasted until four-thirty, with a half-hour break. Ladies from town were furnishing cookies and milk during the breaks. We had the choice of half-pint cartons of chocolate or white milk and homemade peanut butter or chocolate chip cookies. I usually drank white milk, but today chocolate sounded good. It was, and so was the peanut butter cookie.

"Rachel, how was the plane ride?" Winnie asked during the break.

"It was fun. I saw most of the homes of the kids who ride my bus. And the town looks so different from above! I saw your place and Melissa's. What's been going on in town?" I asked. "That's what I'm curious about."

"We've had band practice morning and afternoon,"

Melissa said. "At night we're at home with our families. You haven't missed much."

"Oh!" I couldn't keep the surprise out of my voice. "Anything interesting happen on Saturdays?"

"Like what? We practice on Saturdays, too," Winnie replied.

"Anybody go tobogganing, sledding, skating? Any dances?"

"No dances so far, but last Saturday afternoon after band practice a bunch of us went tobogganing at Cresbard Lake," Melissa said.

"Did Darren go?"

"No, Rachel, he didn't. Don't worry, though. Even if he did, I can tell that he still likes you."

Melissa had told me what I wanted to hear.

After practice, all the kids walked to their respective homes. Carol took a different route back to the hotel so she could walk with a couple of her friends who lived in town. Kim and I tagged along behind. It was getting quite dark by the time we got to the hotel.

At the hotel café, the three of us sat in the middle booth and had the supper special listed on the chalkboard: "Tomato soup/grilled cheese sandwich." It was written in

Mabel's handwriting, and we were the only ones in the café again.

"I wonder what Mom is making for supper tonight," I said.

"They might be having the same as we are," Kim replied.

"This tastes pretty close to Mom's, don't you think?"

"You sound a little homesick, Rachel," Carol said.

"No I'm not. I like it here in town."

We sat, silent for a brief time.

"I can't help but think about them, though. I bet they miss us." *I know they're missing us. All of them.*

Mabel came in to see if we needed anything else. "Dessert tonight?" she asked.

"I'll have an ice cream cone," I said.

"What kind would you like? I have vanilla, chocolate, maple nut, chocolate chip, and strawberry."

"Mmm." Trying to make up my mind. "Maple nut."

"Me, too." Kim said.

"Carol?" Mabel asked.

"Okay."

Mabel scooped up and handed us our cones. Mine first, then Kim's and Carol's. She wrote something, probably adding our cone prices, on the bill.

"Would you like to listen to the radio?" she asked.

"Yeah, that sounds good." *It sounds better than going up to our cold room,* I thought.

Mabel turned on the radio that was sitting on a shelf behind the counter. She turned the dial, but news was on every station. "*The Amos 'n' Andy Music Hall* should be on here soon," she said. "I'll bring some magazines out for you to see."

Mabel returned with some back issues of *Look* magazine and *Newsweek.*

"Here you are, girls."

"Thank you," Carol said, accepting the magazines at the counter and then taking them to our booth.

I took a copy of *Look,* which was much more appealing because it had a lot of pictures compared with *Newsweek*'s news articles in small print. Kim and Carol took copies of *Look,* too. Inside mine were photographs of Queen Elizabeth II of Great Britain. *She's beautiful!* I thought.

"What's that noise?" I asked when I heard a faintly familiar sound from the back living quarters.

We stopped paging through the magazines and listened.

"That's *I Love Lucy*!" I exclaimed. "They have television!"

Kim went behind the counter and reached up to turn

down the radio. We discovered that we could hear the television sounds and voices coming from the living area. We listened and laughed quietly at the antics as though we were hearing it on radio.

"They must be a little hard of hearing that it's on so loud," Kim said.

"I wonder why they don't invite us back there to see it?"

"Because, Rachel, it's their home," Carol explained. "And maybe they don't have enough chairs for three more."

We listened to the whole program and then turned the volume of the radio up when the *Amos 'n' Andy Music Hall* came on. I liked *I Love Lucy* better. The *Amos 'n' Andy* show was a couple of men getting themselves into ridiculous situations with music numbers in between. The *Look* magazine was more interesting, and I returned to it.

At eight o'clock we were tired of sitting in the booth and decided to go to bed.

"Mabel, we're going upstairs now!" Carol called toward the back area.

"Be right out!" Mabel called. A minute later she was at the hallway entrance to the café. "Good night, girls. Let me know if you need anything."

We thanked her, and she turned off the radio. "Get

rested up for school tomorrow," she said as we opened the door to the stairwell.

"We will," we answered. We climbed the chilly stairs and walked down the cold hallway to our room.

In our room, a bit of heat rose through the small grate. To my delight, sound from the television also filtered through the holes. *"See the U.S.A. in your Chevrolet!"* a familiar female voice sang.

"Sounds like Dinah Shore!" Carol said.

Yeah, that's Dinah Shore!

"America is asking you to call," she continued singing. After a man's voice talked about why the car was good, Dinah Shore finished the jingle: *"Drive your Chevrolet through the U.S.A. America's the greatest land of all!"*

"I'm going to wash up and brush my teeth," Carol announced.

"I'm next," Kim said.

"I'm third." I was happy listening to the singing that came through the grate.

"Brrr! That water is cold!" Carol shivered when she returned.

"How come we have to stay here?" Kim complained. "Other kids are staying with families that aren't relatives."

"You know Dad," Carol replied. "He doesn't like to bother other people if he doesn't have to. He doesn't like to be obliged. Besides, he said the hotel is in business to rent rooms and they can use the business, so here we are, and it doesn't do any good to whine about it."

"I like it here in town!" I said.

"Yeah, Mabel's letting you wash up downstairs in the mornings where there's hot water." Kim was a little envious of that.

"She's helping out so it doesn't take us so long to get ready for school. Anyway, I'm the youngest. This is a rare benefit for me. Whenever things involve the three of us, I'm usually last. So this arrangement suits me just fine. You should be grateful that she'll let you and Carol use her tub for your Saturday night baths."

"I'd like to take a bath more often than Saturday night," Kim complained, "but it's too miserable in cold water."

I pulled the quilts back and inched my pajama-clad body between the cold sheets. The weight of the quilts lay heavy on me as I sank into the springy bed.

Kim crawled in on one side, and cold air drifted in. Carol flipped the switch that turned off the ceiling light, and then she raised the window shade halfway. A coating of frost made leafy designs, as though the glass were etched. Dim light from the streetlamp, diffused through the frosty window, would be our nightlight. Our alarm clock would be the morning sun rays beaming through the same window.

"I suppose I have to sleep in the middle," I muttered.

"I want this side," Carol announced, getting in on the other side of me and letting cold air in again. "Besides, Rachel, you are the youngest. Sometimes that has its advantages and sometimes not."

I was sure she had a smug, wise smile on her face.

The three of us lay there in the quiet room. The television had been turned off. The street was quiet, no clock ticked, no voices were heard. Carol moved her feet, and the crinkling of the crisp sheets was amplified by the silence.

"I wonder how Mom and Dad and Susie and Matthew are," I said softly.

"They're probably getting ready for bed, too," Carol replied.

More silence.

"It's not as bad as I thought it would be. The hotel, I mean." I pulled the covers to my chin. "It's clean, and Mabel's nice." I waited for a response. None came.

"I thought it would be scary and dark."

"Shhh."

"It looks scary from the outside."

"Shhh! We have to go to sleep. Tomorrow, school starts again."

"Carol, does being the oldest sometimes have its advantages and sometimes not?"

"Yes. Go to sleep."

"I thought so. Good night."

"Night."

Kim was already asleep. I pulled the covers over my nose and ears, hoping to warm up.

Chapter 20

School was great for a couple weeks. Recess was my favorite time, and I always enjoyed the challenges of schoolwork with Mrs. Kelly. Then the same routine day after day became monotonous. There was school and there was band practice. School and band practice. We had small group sessions throughout the day, and the whole band rehearsed after school and after supper. There was very little time to get together with friends just for the fun of it.

One Friday night, Kim and I arrived at the hotel before Carol.

"This has been a *long* week!" I exclaimed. I dropped my arithmetic book on the booth table and plopped myself on the bench opposite Kim.

"Not so loud. Mabel will hear you," Kim said.

"I don't care. I'm tired of being quiet. I'm tired of being good all the time."

"Do your homework!"

"Don't be so bossy!" I opened my book to the division facts drill page. I wanted to time my speed. I scribbled the answers across a sheet of paper, quickly folded it down, scribbled another row of answers and another row. I made a lot of commotion with an excess of noise.

"For heaven's sake, Rachel! I can't read my history with all that nonsense. What's the matter with you, anyway?"

"I did worse on my timed test today. That's two days in a row!" I pushed my book away in disgust. It hit the salt- and peppershakers, making a loud clink.

"Shhh!" commanded Kim.

"Oh, shhh, yourself!"

Our bickering was stopped by Carol's entrance along with a gust of cold wind. Her mitten-clad hands fumbled with an armload of books. "You'll never guess what I heard today!" she announced. Her books toppled from her arms onto the next booth table.

"No, so I'm not going to guess," Kim said.

"Okay, then," Carol said, and she sat down in the next booth, pretending to ignore us.

"Well, are you going to tell us?" Kim demanded.

"Yeah, are you going to tell us?" I echoed.

"You'll have to beg," she said.

"Is it worth it?" Kim asked.

"Beg!" The smile on her face said it was worth it.

"Okay! Please, pretty please, tell us what you heard today," I begged.

"Not until Kim begs, too."

"All right! Please tell us what you heard," Kim said.

"Beg harder!"

"Please! Pretty, pretty please, tell us!" Kim said louder.

"You mean it?"

"Yes!" There was exasperation in Kim's voice.

"Okay." Carol lowered her voice, probably so Mabel and Frank couldn't hear. "I heard that some kids were playing *strip* poker last night!"

"No! Who?" Kim could not contain her curiosity.

"*What's* strip poker?" I asked.

"You don't know?"

I shook my head. "No."

"Do you know what poker is?" she asked in a condescending tone.

"Yes."

"Do you know what *strip* means?"

"Oh, my!" *That can't be what it is!* "They bet clothes instead of money?"

Carol and Kim nodded.

"And they take off their clothes?" I asked.

"One piece at a time," Kim confirmed.

"Who?" Now I was curious. *Who would do* that?

"Some juniors and seniors."

"*Which* juniors and seniors?" Kim asked.

I was "all ears," as Mom used to say when we kids would listen to conversations that weren't really meant for our ears.

"They didn't tell their names," Carol said.

"Well," Kim said, "then how do you know it's true?"

My jaw still hung open in disbelief.

"Why would anyone start a rumor like that?" Carol asked.

"Nothing else to do," Kim suggested. Then she looked at me. "When are you going to close your mouth, Rachel?"

"Oh." I felt foolish because I hadn't realized that it was open.

"Do you know what else I heard today?" Carol said.

"What will it be this time?" Kim scoffed.

I braced myself.

"We have to go to school on Saturday mornings to make up the days we missed."

"What?" Kim exclaimed. "I wouldn't mind all the school and band practice, but we never have any fun."

"When does it start? Tomorrow?" I asked.

"No. A week from tomorrow."

"Why can't we have a dance or a movie, or something different once in a while?" Kim moaned.

"Well, that's the other thing I have to tell you. There's going to be a school dance tomorrow night," Carol announced.

"Really?" Kim and I exclaimed.

"Finally some good news!" A little cheer had returned to Kim's voice.

"It isn't just for high-schoolers, is it?" I asked.

"No. It's for all grades, but the kids under fifth-grade have to have an older brother or sister with them, or a parent."

"Good!" I replied with considerable relief.

I loved to dance ever since Mrs. Olsen had taught us to square-dance in the third-grade. I shivered with delight at the thought of the dance the next night.

At bedtime, when I was planning what to wear to the

dance, I chose a white sweater and a plaid corduroy skirt that Mom had made for me. Seeing the skirt brought on a guilt attack. Until today, I had been so excited and happy most of the time in town that I forgot about Mom and Dad and Susie and Matthew at home, dealing with the winter all by themselves and missing us.

"I wonder how Mom and Dad are doing," I said aloud. "Do you think Mom is still sick?"

"I hope not," Carol said. "I wonder how Dad is able to do all the chores."

"Do you think they have enough water?" I asked.

"If it didn't freeze," Kim replied.

"I hope none of the cattle got caught in the last snowstorm," Carol said. "The teachers were talking about the cattle that froze to death on a farm north of town."

"Oh, dear!" I said.

"Yeah. Now I feel bad for complaining about not having any fun," Kim said. "Mom and Dad are stuck out there all by themselves with Susie and Matthew. No phone. No television. Only the radio. Lord!"

I promised myself to say an extra prayer at bedtime for Mom and Dad and Susie and Matthew.

Still, I couldn't help being excited about the dance.

Chapter 21

At Saturday's band practice the kids were all aflutter about the dance that night. Everyone was going.

The news that some of the older high school kids had played strip poker was whispered among students of all ages. After our band took a break, Mr. Klitz said that senior Bob Beeber, the lead trombone player, had an announcement to make.

Bob stepped in front of the band, cleared his throat, and said, "There has been a rumor going around that some juniors and seniors played strip poker." Any rustling of sheet music, whispering, or motion stopped instantly. "I've talked to all thirty juniors and seniors, and there are none that have any knowledge of this behavior. We feel this rumor is very unfair to us, and we ask that all discussion of it stop immediately." He looked from one side of the band to the other before he said, "Thank you," and then walked back to his seat.

"Let that be the end of that issue," Mr. Klitz said as he stepped onto his podium.

And it was.

Later, at the hotel, Carol, Kim, and I dressed in our favorite outfits. We told Mabel where we were going and about when we'd be back.

"Have a good time, girls!" she said. "The door will be unlocked for you. Frank and I should still be up at ten o'clock."

We walked cautiously on the sidewalks, not wanting to slip and fall into the snowbanks that still lined the sides. We wore our overshoes, but we didn't put our scarves over our heads, because the wind was not blowing. The sky was filled with stars, and the few lights along the street did not interfere with their brilliance.

Jerry Miner, a high school senior who had his own car and was staying in town with his grandmother, drove near the sidewalk and rolled down his window. "Carol, do you and your sisters want a ride?"

"Sure!" Kim said.

"He asked me," Carol said softly. Then she answered in a louder voice, "Thank you, Jerry. That'd be nice."

"Hop in, then."

Kim was going to get in front, but Carol cleared her throat as she did. She got the message and left the front seat for Carol. Kim and I rode in back.

Jerry looked at Carol with a nice smile, and she smiled back.

Kim looked at me and mouthed, "Hubba-hubba!"

I nodded and smiled.

Carol has a boyfriend, I sang to myself.

Pat Boone was singing "Ain't That a Shame" on the car radio. Jerry turned it down when Carol spoke.

"Everyone's been looking forward to this dance," she said.

"Yeah, it should be fun." He smiled at her again. "We've been working hard in school and band."

In band, Jerry played the tuba and Carol played the baritone horn. The two tuba players were seated behind the three baritone horn players.

"The band sounded good today. Don't you think?" Jerry said.

"We're getting better," Carol replied. "They say practice makes perfect."

"They do," he agreed, with another smile in her direction.

Kim and I looked at each other and rolled our eyes.

Jerry saw me do it in his rearview mirror. That embarrassed me, and I didn't look at Kim the rest of the way, which was only four blocks. We didn't talk, either.

"I'm glad the wind isn't blowing," Carol said.

"Yeah, it isn't half bad tonight." He turned and gave her another smile.

Kim nudged me in the seat.

My return nudge said, *Stop it!* I didn't want to embarrass Carol.

"Here we are," Jerry said, and he parked in front of the schoolyard, where there were a few other cars. Kim and I hurried ahead while Jerry and Carol walked together.

When we entered the door, music from the record player filtered up the stairs from the gym. Kim and I hung our coats on the hooks in the hall. We took off our overshoes and scurried down the stairs.

"Hi, Rachel!" Winnie called.

"Hi, Winnie!" I joined her and several sixth-grade friends already gathered at the middle of the bleachers. I was glad Darren was one of them. Kim went off to find her classmates. Carol joined the sophomores, and Jerry joined the seniors.

Next to the record player at the end of the gym, members of the high school student council held thin, round black records gingerly by the edges without trying to touch the surfaces while they chose the songs to play. Rosemary Clooney was singing, *"Hey there, you with the stars in your eyes,"* and a few high-schoolers were dancing together on the gym floor to the slow rhythm. The beat increased a little when the council chose "Mr. Sandman," sung by the Chordettes.

"Want to dance, Rachel?" Darren asked.

"Okay!"

We walked together onto the floor and danced the two-step.

"Did you walk to school tonight?" Darren asked.

"We started walking, but then Jerry Miner gave us a ride. I think he likes Carol."

"He's dancing with her now," Darren said, and then took steps to turn me so I could see them.

"I think she likes him, too," I said.

When the song was over, Darren and I walked back to the sixth-graders. I danced with David, and even said yes when Lance asked me. He was on his best behavior and didn't say anything to make me angry.

When I got back on the dance floor with Darren, there was a buzz among the students at the record player as a new song, "Heartbreak Hotel" by a singer named Elvis Presley, burst out. The beat was fast and the guitar whined *twang, twang* in just the right places to emphasize the singer's sorrow over losing his girlfriend.

Some of the high school kids on the dance floor began to really move. As they jitterbugged, they mixed in motions from their shoulders and their hips. Darren and I watched their animated moves. There was something about the music and its beat that summoned me.

"What do you think, Rachel? Shall we try that?" Darren asked.

"I *like* the beat! Let's do it!"

The gym floor was full of couples swinging, twirling, and shaking. The rhythm was terrific. On the sideline, many of the kids looked surprised.

Darren and I were laughing and having a good time dancing that way.

"Rachel!" Carol snapped from behind. Her sharp reprimand surprised me.

"Rachel, stop that!" she demanded in a whisper. "Don't dance like that!"

We stopped, and poor Darren stood there, embarrassed. He didn't know what to do.

"But it's fun! The beat is great!" I insisted.

"Go sit down!" she ordered, again in a low voice so she wouldn't attract attention. I could tell that Jerry was embarrassed, too.

"No!" I insisted.

Suddenly the music stopped. And so did the dancing. A teacher chaperone had raised the needle arm and set it over on the armrest. "There will be no Elvis Presley played here tonight!" he declared.

"Ooh," the crowd moaned.

"See!" Carol said smugly, and she walked back to the bleachers. Jerry shrugged and followed her.

"Now find something else to play if you want the dance to go on!" the chaperone ordered.

"I told you they wouldn't let us play Elvis," one girl said.

"Well, we gave it a try," a boy replied.

The next songs were pretty mild: "Ain't That a Shame," "Yellow Rose of Texas," "Little Things Mean a Lot."

When "We're Gonna Rock Around the Clock," with its fast beat, started playing, I expected a chaperone to come and lift the needle again before the end of *"We're gonna rock, rock, rock 'til broad daylight!"*

I was dancing with Darren again, and I said, "Oh, my, do you think they'll stop this one?"

"We'll dance till they do," Darren said.

"Where's Carol?"

"She's sitting on the bleachers, watching you."

"Well, if she wants to stop me, she'll have to come and make a scene."

We jitterbugged on, and so did all the others, until the end of the song.

I caught a glimpse of Carol on the bleachers, glaring at me in disapproval.

"I guess that song meets the chaperones' approval. I wonder why 'Heartbreak Hotel' doesn't."

"Who knows!" Darren said.

The last dance of the evening was to "Three Coins in the

Fountain." It was traditional that the last dance was danced with your date or your favorite friend. I waited to see if Darren would ask me. He did. While we danced to the slow tempo of the song, I saw Carol dancing with Jerry, and Kim was dancing with Devon. You could tell they were just friends.

"That was fun. Thank you, Rachel," Darren said. It was polite or "proper etiquette," as Mrs. Kelly had pointed out in a dance class, for the boy to thank the girl for the dance.

"You're welcome. See you Monday at school."

"Yeah!"

"Good night, Winnie! Good night, Melissa!" I called to them before I ran to catch up with Kim, who was following Carol and Jerry up the stairs.

"Are you giving us a ride home, Jerry?" Kim asked.

"Sure am!" he said.

Carol was miffed and didn't speak to me.

When we stopped at the hotel and the three of us opened our doors to get out, Jerry said, "Can I talk to you for a minute, Carol?"

"Oh! Okay!" she said. "I'll be right in," she told us.

"I bet he wants to kiss her," Kim whispered to me.

"Do you really think so?" I whispered back.

"We'll peek out the window when we get in."

Kim and I slid into the opposite sides of the booth next to the window. Each of us moved the far bottom corners of the curtains just a little so we could see out.

"He has his arm on the back of the seat," Kim reported.

"It looks like he's sliding over closer to her," I said.

"He is! Oooh, that's the first move."

"How do you know it's the first move?" I asked.

"Haven't you ever been to the movies?"

"His arm is around her."

"Second move," Kim chirped.

"He's pulling her toward him!"

"Third move."

"They're kissing!"

"And so they are!" Kim smiled.

"Do you think Mom and Dad would care?" I asked.

"I don't think so. She is sixteen, and Jerry's a nice boy. Besides, Mom and Dad aren't here."

"Yeah, but they wouldn't want us to do anything they wouldn't want us to do normally," I reasoned. "Did you see her get mad at me for dancing to the Elvis Presley song?"

"I saw that."

"She acted like I'd committed a crime."

"How do you think Mom and Dad would feel about you dancing like that?" she asked.

"There wasn't anything wrong with it. The music has a terrific beat, and it felt good to move around."

Just then, Jerry jumped out of his door and walked around to open Carol's for her.

"Quick! Here she comes! Act like we don't know a thing," Kim said.

I leaned my back against the window wall and stretched my legs out on my bench. Kim followed suit.

"What are you two doing?" Carol asked when she came in the door.

"Nothing," we lied.

"Were you looking out the window?"

"Why?" Kim asked.

"No reason," she said, pretending that nothing had happened.

"It's past our bedtime, so we'd better go up," she said.

Kim and I followed her. Kim nudged me with her elbow. I nudged back. Our big sister had a boyfriend.

"Did you have a good time at the dance, Carol?" Kim asked as we were getting ready for bed.

"Yes, it was fun. But I was disappointed in you, Rachel."

"There was nothing to be disappointed about. Besides, you're not my boss."

"Oh, yes, I am. Because I'm the oldest, Mom and Dad expect me to be in charge."

"I'm not a baby, so stop watching me like a mother hawk."

That seemed to be the end of the discussion for the night.

When I folded the skirt that Mom had made me and placed it in the drawer, I thought of her and Dad at home, and I felt guilty for having had so much fun at the dance.

Poor Susie must be so lonely for us. They all must be. I wonder what Matthew thinks with all of us gone? And Mom? Dear God, please don't let her still be sick.

We put on our pajamas, took turns brushing our teeth in the cold water across the hall, and climbed beneath the quilts. I was in the middle again — like peanut butter stuck between two slices of bread.

Before I fell asleep, I felt a yearning for my bedroom at home — and for Susie, Mom and Dad, and Matthew.

Oh, my word! I'm homesick!

Chapter 22

One Saturday morning after school, Carol, Kim, and I were walking to the hotel.

"What a long morning!" I said.

"I know," Kim agreed.

"Why do these Saturday mornings seem so hard?" I asked. "It's only the second one we've had."

"Would you rather be home feeding cattle?" Carol asked.

"Today, I think I'd rather be home, but not necessarily feeding cattle."

"Careful!" Carol warned as she led the way on the snow-packed sidewalk. The bright sunshine on this early March day made the snow slick beneath our overshoes.

It was also perfect for making snowballs. We were just past a long, slippery stretch when a *whoosh* and a *plop* reached my ears. A snowball had sailed between Kim and me and dropped ahead of us.

"Who threw that snowball?" Kim demanded, turning around.

"I did!" Devon answered, forming another one. David was walking in the street with him. They were staying at their aunt and uncle's in town.

Soon we were embroiled in a snowball fight. Us against them. Well, Kim and I against them. Carol was too ladylike to throw snowballs.

I ducked the snowballs as they zipped toward me. Turning my back for protection, I started stockpiling my own ammunition. I waited until one of them was in range and then hurled the snowballs.

"Bull's-eye!" I had hit David smack center in his chest. *Now, he's out to get me!* I ran behind a pile of snow and furtively made more snowballs. I planned to bombard him mercilessly when he rounded the pile.

"Ah!" I yelled in surprise when attackers charged from both sides of the pile. Dick Mackey had joined the fight. He and David thrust a snowball at me. I huddled, head down to protect my face and my precious stockpile. As they backed away laughing, I let them have it. I threw only one at David and hit him just below the white patch from the last one. The next three I hurled at Dick with all my might. Wham! on the arm. Wham! on the chest. Wham! on the back.

"So you want to play rough, do you?" He packed a snowball and flung it at me. I felt the pain in my neck; then I toppled to the ground and lay still — very still.

"I saw that!" Carol shouted at Dick. She ran and knelt by me. "Rachel? Rachel?" Carol turned me over, nestled my head in her arms, and pulled my scarf back onto my head. "Look what you've done! Rachel? Rachel? Say something!"

"What are we going to do, Carol?" Kim asked, hovering near.

"It was just a snowball," Dick protested. "I didn't throw it that hard."

"Did it hit her in the head?" Devon asked.

"No, her neck." Dick shook his head in disbelief. "How could this happen from getting hit in the neck?"

"I don't know," Devon replied.

"Shall I run and get our aunt?" David asked.

"No, I'll go," Devon said.

"Better hurry," I said, a wide, satisfied smile crossing my face. I opened my eyes and sat up. I glared at Dick and then Devon. "How does it feel?"

"Rachel! You scared us to death! How could you fake something like that?" Carol snapped.

"Remember that trick *they* pulled on David and me with the tramp in the barn?"

"Yeah!" David grinned, almost as pleased as I was. "Good one, Rachel! Good one!"

"Okay, okay, we deserved it," Devon conceded.

"But *we* didn't," Carol said, pointing to Kim and herself.

"I'm sorry for scaring *you*, but we owed them, didn't we, David?"

"Yes, we did."

Chapter 23

The cold continued. Heavy snowfalls. High winds. It was the winter that wouldn't go away.

There would be a couple of nice days when the sun would shine and the temperature would warm a little and get our hopes up. Then a blast of arctic air would collide with the warm temperatures and another heavy snowfall would result.

After the snowfall, farmers who lived near town would clear their roads with their farmhand shovels and then help remove snow from the town's streets. A day later, it was almost certain that the wind would blow those streets shut again.

There were some days when the wind was so strong and the weather so dangerous that school was delayed until the wind died down. On mornings when the wind howled and frost on our hotel window obscured the world outside, I dreaded hearing the telephone ring downstairs.

"Oh no!" I moaned one morning when it did. "I bet that's a school delay. I hope it's not for *all* day!"

We couldn't hear what Mabel was saying on the phone through the grate. We had to wait for the message until she climbed the stairs and knocked on our door.

"Girls, there won't be any school this morning for sure," she called through the door.

"Thank you, Mabel!" Carol called back from bed.

"You can come down for breakfast whenever you want."

"Thank you, Mabel," Carol said again.

"Mabel's nice," I said.

"Yep, she is," Carol said.

"Are you awake, Kim?" I asked. We hadn't heard from her side of the bed.

"No, I'm still asleep."

"Then you're talking in your sleep."

"Rachel . . . Rachel . . . can you hear me?" Kim said in a weird voice, like I'd heard in a spooky movie when a fortuneteller pretended to talk to a dead person.

I played along. "Yes, I hear you."

"Get out of bed . . . and walk to the window."

"No! You'll probably tell me to jump out the window."

"Walk to the window . . . and then jump out the window. Someone is waiting there to catch you."

"Go jump out the window yourself!"

"Someone is waiting . . . I can see . . . why, it's Darren!"

"Oh, shut up!" I tried to shove her out of bed with my feet, but I wasn't strong enough.

She laughed a spooky laugh.

"Stop it, you two!" Carol said.

I lifted my arm out of the covers to test the temperature. "Brrrr! It's cold this morning." I pulled my arm back under the covers immediately.

The wind blew through the sides of a loose-fitting storm window, and the vibration created a moaning whistle.

"I hate the thought of leaving this warm spot," Carol said.

"You're the oldest. You have to leave first," I said.

"Kim?" I questioned again.

"I'm still sleeeeping."

The three of us lay quiet for a while.

Eventually the radio was turned on downstairs and it was loud enough so that we could hear the weather report through the grate.

"A strong wind from the north will prevail today. Expect gusts as high as forty miles per hour. The wind will subside tonight, with temperatures falling near zero. Tomorrow will be sunny and mild, with a high of thirty degrees."

"Zeeero!" Kim said in her weird voice. Carol and I ignored her.

The announcer continued: "Tomorrow, if conditions permit, state and county plows will work on those roads respectively. Rural residents living on township roads are asked to be responsible for clearing their roads leading to the state and county roads."

"I'm sure Dad has cleared the township road to our lane every time there's been a break in the weather," Carol said. "You know how he always likes to be ready and get an early jump on things."

I pictured Dad in his big parka, with the hood up and the flap snapped across his face, driving home on the cleared road, when suddenly the wind whipped up and tried to blow him off the seat of the tractor. The wind could undo in a matter of hours what it took him a day, or even days, to do.

Mom, with a worried frown, would keep tabs on his progress and his welfare from the large west window. Susie would, too.

Unexpectedly, I felt mopey and melancholy.

"Do you think Mom is still sick?" I asked. For some reason I felt a little ache in my stomach.

Carol replied, "If it's morning sickness caused by pregnancy, then it often goes away after a few months."

"I *hope* it's gone away. I can't imagine being sick in this awful winter, stuck out in the country," I said.

We were silent. None of us mentioned our feelings about having another baby.

"It's been a long time since we've seen them," I said.

"Yes," Carol said softly. "It's been seven weeks."

None of us moved for a while.

I thought about my warm room at home, the sky blue walls, the sun shining through the east window — as much of it as could get through the blowing snow — Susie in bed all by herself, the table half empty during mealtimes. That scene changed to the raging wind and the blizzard and Dad, *oh, my,* walking into a wind that wanted to prevent him from feeding and watering his cattle.

Carol's voice interrupted that scene. "Well, we should probably get up."

"Why?" Kim asked. She had changed back to her normal voice.

"For one reason, it's not fair to Mabel to have breakfast too late," Carol said.

"I'm ready," I said. I didn't relish the idea of facing the cold air, but I didn't want to think any more about Dad in the blizzard and Mom being sick and Susie and Matthew missing us.

"Now *I* don't want to leave this warm spot," Kim said.

"Well, just a few minutes," Carol said.

"What do you guys want for breakfast?" I asked.

"Shhh, Rachel!" Kim said.

"I'm tired of lying here! I'm going to get up and *I'll* go down and order for us," I said. "Carol, *may* I?" I asked sarcastically.

"Okay, Kim, let's get up," Carol said.

"All right!" she said, as if she were rolling her eyes.

We braved the chilly room, dressed, and went down for breakfast. As usual, no one else was in the café. Only once did we share the restaurant with another diner, and that was one night during a snowstorm when a truck driver was stranded. He ordered *three* hamburgers, french fries, and coffee.

We took our time eating the Cream of Wheat we had all agreed to have. The hot cereal and the warm temperature in the café lifted my spirits. After breakfast we stayed inside the café. Kim and I played checkers while Carol finished reading a history assignment.

By late morning, the wind went down and I waited for the telephone to ring. When it did, I prayed, *Please let there be school. Please let there be school.*

"School will start at one o'clock today, girls," Mabel reported.

Thank goodness!

We had classes from one until four o'clock, a cookie-and-milk break, and then band practice until five-thirty.

It was a rigorous rehearsal. We were still working on "Rhapsody in Blue," and there were some tough parts for Melissa, Cara Moser, and me. We were third chair coronets and had less experience in playing our horns than most of the band members.

During practice, Mr. Klitz tapped his baton on his stand and said, "Third chair coronets, let's try those last two lines again."

We did, and made some errors in counting.

"Again!" he said.

We flubbed up once more.

"I think I'll have you three come back after supper to work on this piece," he said. "Can you do that?"

We all nodded, embarrassed.

Then he addressed the whole band. "Let's try it again from the top of the page." He winced slightly and shook his head when we played through the tough part.

At five-thirty Mr. Klitz tapped his baton on the stand for the last time and then said, "Have a good night, kids. See you tomorrow, except for the third chair coronets. I'll see you tonight at seven."

We nodded again. We weren't going to forget.

"I am so tired of playing 'Rhapsody in Blue' over and over!" I said to Carol and Kim on the way to the hotel. "And now I have to go back and play it over and over again."

"Rachel, the whole band has to sound good together," Carol said. "You can't have noticeable mistakes when the band plays in Chicago."

"You aren't going to get any sympathy from me," said Kim. "I've been practicing my horn for two years longer than you have."

"But you weren't going to *Chicago* two years ago, either!" I replied.

On cold nights like this, I wished the hotel were closer than five blocks from school. For three of those five blocks I had to traipse into the north wind. It wasn't raging, but any wind from the north is cold in the winter.

The seven o'clock practice session turned out to be more tedious than I had anticipated. Mr. Klitz had us play the challenging parts of "Rhapsody in Blue" over and over and over. I began to feel weary, and tears suddenly welled up in my eyes. I couldn't hold them back, making it impossible to see the swimming notes on the sheet of music. Teardrops rolled down my cheeks. I was embarrassed and didn't want anyone to know that I was crying, so I kept on playing rather than stop to wipe them away.

My flubs became so obvious that Mr. Klitz, sitting by us, tapped his pen on the music stand, signaling us to stop. He was about to say something, but he must have seen my tears. Instead, he announced softly, "That's probably enough for tonight. You girls can go. We'll work on this another time."

Melissa took a tissue from her pocket and gently handed it to me. I nodded my thanks and wiped my cheeks dry and then dabbed my eyes with it. I blew my nose, and it sounded so loud in the quiet band room.

I was relieved that practice was over but embarrassed by my tears, because I didn't know why I was crying.

The hotel café was a welcome refuge. Carol and Kim were playing a card game called hearts.

"How was practice?" Carol asked.

"Okay," I lied. "Do you think I could order some hot cocoa? I'm cold and hungry."

"Why don't you go back and ask Mabel?" Carol suggested.

"No, I don't feel like it. It's not like she's *Mom*."

Tears formed, and I tried so hard to stop them so they wouldn't roll down my face. *Not again!* I thought.

"Rachel's crying!" Kim said.

"Don't you feel well?" Carol asked.

"I'm fine," I said.

Carol got up from the booth and walked into the hallway leading to the Stewarts' living quarters. She knocked on the wall at the end and called, "Mabel?"

Mabel came to the doorway. "Yes?"

"Do you think you could make some cocoa for Rachel? She just got back from section practice and is a little cold and hungry."

"Of course! I'll make some for all three of you."

"Thank you very much," Carol said.

When Mabel brought the hot cocoa, with whipped cream floating on top, the aroma from the steaming, sweet drink made my mouth water.

"Thank you," we said.

I smiled my gratitude to her and to Carol.

Chapter 24

There was a break from blizzards and drifting snow for about a week after that. Cars and pickups came to town to stock up on supplies that were finally delivered to the grocery stores.

On Saturday evening, Carol went out with Jerry to a party for a few of their high school friends at Gretchen's house. Kim and I stayed at the hotel and listened to the radio. During the local news, we heard the update on the progress of clearing area roads.

"The break in the harsh weather this week has allowed snowplows to work round the clock at opening the main roads. The following highways are open to two-way traffic: Highways 81, 20, 45, and 212 in this region. Most county roads leading to Faulkton, Cresbard, Chelsea, and Wecota are open, but many spots are still only one lane wide. For those folks between Highways 20 and 212 on the Miranda road, there is a breakdown in the plow clearing that county road and it will be some time before that road is opened."

"Of all the roads, it would *have* to be the road that leads to our place!" I moaned. "When do you think Mom and Dad are going to be able to get out? We don't even know if they are sick or dead or alive!"

"They're not dead," Kim said. "Don't be foolish."

"I'm not foolish!"

"You're foolish . . . and you're dumb!"

"I don't think it's dumb to worry about my family. Why do you always have to put me down?"

Kim paused for a few seconds, then answered, "Because you're younger than I am."

"You're younger than Carol, but Carol doesn't do that to you."

"Carol doesn't have to. Carol is perfect in everything. She's pretty, she's smart, she's at the top of her class, she's mature."

"So you're picking on me because you're jealous of Carol?"

Kim thought for a minute. "Maybe," she conceded.

"I don't pick on Susie because I'm jealous of you!"

"Hah! What makes you jealous of me?"

"Well . . . you're better at running all the farm machines than I am. Dad brags about the way you can handle the combine and harvest the grains. I don't run the combine. Carol doesn't run the combine. Even Mom doesn't. Just you and Dad."

"Yeah, that's true," Kim said, nodding.

"You swim! The rest of us are afraid of the water. So *you* help Dad fix the fences that cross the creek. And he brags about that."

"Yeah! Okay. Anything else?"

"Yes. You're neat and tidy and organized, and I'm messy. Look in your drawer upstairs. All of your things are folded neatly in orderly piles. Then look at my drawer."

A slight smile crossed her face. "You are kind of messy," she said.

She was silent for a few seconds, and then she spoke softly. What she said surprised me. "You know you're not dumb. I shouldn't have said that. And you're not foolish."

A sense of relief came over me. "I'm glad you didn't really mean it," I said.

"Truce?" she asked.

"Truce."

Then it was time for *Gunsmoke,* a favorite program of mine. But I didn't really follow the story. I was contemplating what Kim and I had just said.

Being sisters is complicated, I thought.

I started to miss my other sister, who was probably also missing me eight miles away, where, according to the radio, she was still snowed in with Mom and Dad and Matthew.

The next day was church, and Carol, Kim, and I would again fill only a small section of our family's usual pew. The thought of going to church another Sunday without the whole family made me feel sad. At bedtime, it seemed that I could barely lift my feet to the next stair. In bed, I lay awake for a long time, thinking and worrying about home.

The next morning, as we walked down the stairs on our way to church, I heard a car pull up and then a car door.

"Do you think they're ready?" a high-pitched voice asked. I knew that voice!

"Susie?" I exclaimed, and rushed out the door.

"Susie! It *is* you!" I was going to say, *Mom! Dad!* too, but Susie ran to me and hugged me so tight that I couldn't.

"Rachel! I missed you!" she said, still hugging me.

"I missed you, too, Susie!"

"How could you make it in?" I asked Dad as he got out of his door. "The radio said that the snowplow was broken down and our county road isn't open."

"They may have borrowed a snowplow or found one somewhere, because we saw the plow go by last night and decided to make a run to town to check on you girls and go to church today." Dad talked as he went around the car to take Matthew from Mom's arms so she could get out. I was surprised at how much bigger Matthew looked.

I watched anxiously as Mom got out of the car and stood up. *Will she look sick?*

"Mom!" I ran to her and threw my arms around her, as far around her as they would go. Tears of relief filled my eyes.

She was my beautiful dark-haired mother again, even if her stomach stuck out noticeably under her coat.

"I missed you, Mom."

"I missed you, too, Rachel." She took a quick swipe at the tears wetting her cheeks. "And I missed you, Kim. And you, Carol." She hugged them each in turn. Then they hugged Susie.

Dad stood nearby, holding Matthew, who smiled and

pointed at us while the women of our family reconnected. Then we took turns holding Matthew.

"Matthew, you've gained weight!" I exclaimed. He laughed when I buzz-kissed his chubby cheek.

We hugged Dad, too, who usually resisted gestures of affection.

"Time to get to church," he said.

He and Mom had not been to church for eleven weeks. Kim, Carol, and I had gone every Sunday. Our little frame church was only two blocks from the hotel, one north and one west on the farthest street west of town.

This Sunday our church pew was complete. Dad, Mom — in her lovely navy blue maternity outfit designed to camouflage her large stomach — holding Matthew, and Susie, me, Kim, and Carol in our stair-step order. Other pews were also more occupied this Sunday than past Sundays.

While only half listening to the sermon, I hatched a brilliant idea. When I got into the car after Sunday school, I asked, "May we pretty please go home today?"

Dad and Mom looked at each other. My hopes soared when I saw them smile.

"I don't see why not," Dad said. "We'll arrange it with Mabel. You'll come home today, and I'll bring you in to school tomorrow. The weather's supposed to hold another day."

At the hotel, Carol, Kim, and I quickly changed from our church clothes to the pants we wore on the plane ride.

One last stop before leaving town was Mel's Market, which was open so people going to church could get supplies. Mom got flour, sugar, yeast, laundry detergent, canned milk, powdered milk, baby food, ice cream, and Velveeta cheese.

Driving on the county road between Highway 20 and Miranda, I realized that Mom and Dad had taken a chance coming to town. The one plowed lane was narrow, and some spots were icy from melted snow that froze overnight. Our Oldsmobile was a big car, and the extra weight of us kids in the back made the trip home easier.

In our yard, the heaps of snow were smaller than when we had left. The haystacks were considerably lower, too. At that moment, I was sure I could smell the dried alfalfa.

"Hey, can I feed the cattle?" I couldn't believe that those words came out of my mouth.

"Did you hear that, Kid? Rachel wants to know if she can feed the cattle!"

Mom laughed, then asked, "Are you going to let her?"

"Well, I don't know. She's probably a softy after living in town all those weeks." He winked at her. "On the other hand, I'll take all the help I can get."

Blackie came out of the chicken coop to greet us as we drove up. "I bet you missed us, too, didn't you, boy?" I asked, stroking the top of his head. The gratitude in his eyes and the wagging of his tail said yes.

Before I entered the house, I checked to see that my work clothes were where I had left them in the garage. All were there except my cowboy boots.

"Has anyone seen my cowboy boots?" I asked.

"They're in our room," Susie answered.

"What are my boots doing in here?" I asked after seeing them in the corner of the bedroom.

"I wear them sometimes," Susie confessed.

"Why?"

"Mommy says they're getting too small for you."

"They are, but you can't have them until I get a new pair."

"Can't I wear them sometimes? Pretty please?"

Her innocent, pleading eyes softened me. "Oh, all right," I said as I squeezed my feet into my boots and felt the toes squashed at the tip.

I put on my work clothes — not so many layers needed today — and headed for the cattle yard. Blackie accompanied me, but at the gate, I told him, "Stay!" so he wouldn't agitate the cattle.

I climbed the haystack and pitched the dry, sweet-smelling alfalfa down the sides. It was sunny and calm, with clear blue skies. I leaned on the pitchfork, surveying the endless white landscape — not menacing, tranquil — on a day like this.

I found a dip in the haystack and lay on my back with my eyes closed, the sun warming my face and my spirit.

Another warming awaited me when I returned to the house: the aromas and tastes of Mom's Sunday dinner, which included a savory, perfectly browned beef roast with mashed potatoes and gravy, and all of us around the table, together again.

I purposely did not think of the conversation between two farmers I had overheard on the way out of church. "The radio says we're supposed to get another blast of winter on Tuesday!"

"Sounds like we're in for another couple of bad weeks!" was the reply.

Epilogue

We returned to the hotel the next day, and winter did rage for another two weeks. But then the warm weather finally hit. Creeks and rivers flooded as the enormous amounts of melted snow raced to fill their beds. That meant our own Snake Creek overflowed its banks, washing out the bridge and the curve in the road, stranding Mom, Dad, Susie, and Matthew for another couple of weeks.

Since there were no hard-topped surface roads leading to town, all the roads in the vicinity were muddy quagmires — even the graveled ones.

Heavy trucks had gouged deep ruts in the thawed Highway 20 before the trucks were banned. When the roadbed dried, the ruts presented hazardous travel for cars and pickups. Major road repair was required.

Farmers living near town had volunteered to remove the piled snow from the streets to prevent them from becoming slushy canals, which would have been nasty for students and motorists to navigate. Therefore, the spring thaw wasn't as difficult for us in town as it was for those on the farms.

By late April, the Snake Creek had retreated to its bed, content to wind rapidly through our farm and over the spillway of the reconstructed dam, to the next farm.

Carol, Kim, and I were back home after twelve weeks in town, riding the bus to school with a delighted Susie.

One afternoon when we returned home from school, no one was there. Later that evening, Dad returned with Matthew, but not Mom. She was in the Faulkton hospital with their new baby daughter, our new sister, Lynette.

The long hours committed to band rehearsals that winter and spring, and again in the fall of my seventh-grade year, paid off in December at the Midwest Band Clinic in Chicago. The newspapers there gave us a glowing report and called our band the outstanding favorite.

Ironically, we traveled the seven hundred miles by train — in a snowstorm.

Afterword

In keeping with the time sequence of *Prairie Summer* (1954) and *Lessons* (1954–55), two previous books about Rachel Johnson and her family, *Prairie Winter* was set in 1955–56.

Many of the adventures in this story are true, inspired by my memories of the big winter of 1951–52 in South Dakota. Snowstorm after snowstorm blew through. My oldest sister did start walking to town for the basketball game. Our school bus really stalled, and we stayed at Joe and Vi Holt's farm for several days. One of those days included the "tramp" prank pulled on Rachel and David. Eventually my father came bravely through to take us home with the tractor, and when the snow kept us from school altogether, Herbert Cowhick flew us into town, and we stayed at the Cresbard Hotel as described. Spring flooding and muddy roads, the aftermath of a big winter, continued to challenge our patience and endurance until summer came.

Our family *never* had a phone on the farm. My father finally conceded and had a phone installed in Mom's and his apartment approximately fifteen years after retiring to a nearby city.